# WAR OF THE NOSES

## A NORA BLACK MIDLIFE PSYCHIC MYSTERY BOOK THREE

## RENEE GEORGE

BARKSIDE OF THE MOON PRESS

War of the Noses

A Nora Black, Midlife Psychic Book 3

Print edition: August 2020

ISBN: 978-1-947177-36-9

240 pages

Publisher: Barkside of the Moon Press

"Sense & Scent Ability is everything! Nora Black is sassy, smart, and her smell-o-vision is scent-sational. I can't wait for the next Nora book!

*For My BFFs.*
*You are the reasons I can write best friends who really have each*
*others' backs! I love you!*

## ACKNOWLEDGMENTS

A huge thank you to BFFs Robbin, Michele, and Robyn for diligently reading through this story multiple times. You helped me make it so great! Thank you for being my people! I love you guys!

To my editor Kelli Collins. You are a great friend and my rock! I'm sorry I am such a crap client. LOL (The woman is a saint, people!)

To the PWF #13 - Thanks for bringing attention to heroines of a certain age. You ladies are magnificent.

My husband Steve and my son Taylor for taking up the slack around the house, and most of all, leaving me alone to write! I literally couldn't do this without you.

My BFF Dakota Cassidy for being my one true heart when it comes to all things bingeworthy. I love you, girl!

And finally, to the readers. You are making this midlife writer happier than you can even imagine! Thank you for loving Nora and going on this journey with her and her BFF brigade.

**My name is Nora Black. I'm turning fifty-two, but I don't feel a day over thirty-nine. That is, when my feet don't hurt, my eyesight isn't failing, and my scent-induced psychic ability isn't showing me crimes.**

For my birthday, my best friends Gilly and Pippa signed us up for a weekend at the Central Midwest Spa Convention. Yay. Massages, fine dining, maid service, and best of all, as long as we attend a few workshops, the weekend is a tax write-off. It should be all sunshine and roses, right? Wrong.

My former intern at Belliza Beauty, aka the Job Stealer, Carmen Carraway, is a featured presenter. Yuck. Throw in an ex-boyfriend, a number one fan, a brewing scandal, and a dead body, and my relaxing birthday weekend is DOA.

I'll need all my senses, along with my friends, if I want to stop a killer from striking once again.

# CHAPTER 1

*Thursday, August 7th...*

"I'm gonna miss you," Ezra said as he nuzzled my ear.

I giggled. "It's only for four days." I turned in his arms and leaned into his kisses. "But I'm going to miss you, too."

It had been a few months since he'd first declared his love for me over Memorial Weekend. Now it was August, and every day with him this summer had made me happier than I could've imagined. Not that I had thought finding love after fifty was impossible, I just hadn't thought it could feel so exciting and brand new again.

"I hate missing your birthday." His emerald-green gaze mesmerized me. "But I'm glad you're getting away with Gilly and Pippa. Even if it's a work thing."

"Hardly work." I smiled. Gilly, Pippa, and I were headed to the annual Central Midwest Spa Convention in the city for a girls' weekend of relaxation and reconnection. Gilly had booked us massages for late this afternoon, facials and mani-pedis on Friday, and I was looking forward to seeing all my old friends and clients, and bonus, dressing up as a flapper for the Roaring Twenties dinner party on Saturday evening.

Ezra cupped my neck, his fingers entwining my hair and diverting my thoughts from the beauty biz to him. "Call me tonight."

"Promise," I said as he pressed his forehead against mine.

"You two need to stop canoodling and get to packing up the damn vehicle," Gilly Martin, my BFF since kindergarten, said as she dragged a large suitcase, her second one, down to the curb from her house.

The house right next to mine.

The thought made me smile. I had closed four weeks ago on the ranch home in Gilly's cul-de-sac. Mr. Garner, the previous owner, had moved away from Garden Cove after a short stint in jail for assault with a deadly weapon and withholding evidence from the police. He'd been a sweet man, who'd lost his way when his daughter had disappeared. I'd helped him find the truth about his girl, and he'd shown his gratitude by selling me the house under market value. I'd offered him more, but he'd been ready to move on. I missed his beagle, Godiva, who I'd taken care of while the older man had been incarcerated, but I was glad she was back with her furdad.

"Our bags are already in the trunk," I said, referring to mine and Pippa's suitcases. "As yours would be if you had packed last night like I suggested."

"I don't operate that way," Gilly quipped. She smacked my butt cheek as she passed me on the way to the SUV

Pippa had rented for our trip. She wore khaki chinos, a sage-green tank top, and a bright pink pair of tennis shoes. The ensemble accentuated and flattered her curves.

As I watched Gilly try to manage her luggage, I didn't attempt to keep the incredulity from my voice. "For someone who waited until the last minute, you sure packed a lot of stuff. How many suitcases do you have? It's a good thing we got a sports vehicle. As it is, I might have to ride on your lap."

"You're," Gilly hauled up the first bag and loaded it into the hatchback, "being," she grunted as she shoved the second bag on top of the first, "dramatic."

"I don't think you are," Ezra whispered. "Did she pack her entire closet?"

"And her entire dresser," I answered.

Gilly touched the button on the hatch.

It lowered then raised.

I chuckled.

She frowned and pushed it again.

It lowered then raised. She clenched her fists and let out a noise of frustration. "It won't flippin' close."

Pippa Davenport, my other best friend, came out Gilly's front door wagging her finger. "I told her she packed too much damn stuff." Pippa—dressed in designer jeans, strappy sandals, and a pale pink scoop-neck shirt— had arrived an hour earlier to have coffee and to help light a fire under Gilly's butt. She brushed her mid-length blonde hair off her shoulders. At thirty-six years old, she was the youngest in our group. Even so, over the years that I'd known her, she had perfected the stare of a disappointed parent. She turned that look on Gilly. "Now, get it in the trunk or get it out."

"That's what she said," I joked quietly. Ezra chuckled.

"But I need it," Gilly whined. "I need all of it."

Pippa looked unconvinced. "For one weekend?"

It was technically a four-day event, opening today, which was Thursday, with events going through Sunday morning, but Pippa wasn't wrong. Gilly had packed way too much for our short trip.

Gilly didn't agree. "One suitcase is for clothes, one for shoes and snacks, and the carry-on bag has my makeup and hair stuff in it. What would you like me to leave behind, Pippa? My curling iron? My trail mix? My under-wear?" She was getting herself worked up.

"Calm down, Norma Rae," I said, pulling away from Ezra and heading down to the SUV. I took out the bags, all four of them—two Gilly's, one mine, one Pippa's—plus the small carryon and, with some effort, reorganized the larger bags sideways so that they slid in next to each other. I put the carryon bag on its side and placed it on top. I stepped back, hit the button, and the hatch closed completely. I looked at Gilly. "*Voíla.*"

She smiled triumphantly back at me. "See. I told you they would fit."

"Only because I've been the reigning champion of Tetris since 1984." I looked at my smartwatch. Eight thousand and thirteen steps since I'd gotten up this morning at six a. m., pulse seventy-two, and the time was ten-fifteen now. "Damn it. We have to go." I looked back at Ezra with a sigh.

"Hey," said Pippa. "That should be, yay, we get to go.

You can live without Ezra for a weekend. You don't see me getting all sappy about leaving Jordy."

"Yeah," Gilly agreed. "I didn't plan this weekend for you to be a big fuddy-dud. So, no pining for Detective Hot Stuff. We are going to have a great time."

"Is it okay if Detective Hot Stuff pines for Nora?" Ezra asked.

"Absolutely." I sealed my response with a kiss before patting his chest in lieu of goodbye.

As much as I'd miss Ezra's company, I was happy to be getting away from work and Garden Cove for a few days with my BFFs. Besides, I'd loved going to the expos and conventions when I worked as the regional sales manager for Belliza Beauty. Every year the company came out with new and exciting cutting-edge skincare lines, makeup, and hair care. Barbara DeMonde, the sales director for Chromorphia Cosmetics and my former college roommate, was the keynote speaker for the main event on Saturday, and I couldn't wait to see her.

I smiled at both Gilly and Pippa. "We're going to have a killer time."

\* \* \*

"THIS WEEKEND IS GOING TO SUCK," I said as we made our way through the lobby of the Frazier Ambassador Hotel a little after noon. On a billboard near the convention registration table was an announcement that Carmen Carraway, the younger viper of a woman who had taken my job as regional sales manager for Belliza Beauty, was the keynote speaker for the Beauty Trends event on Saturday.

"I thought Barbara DeMonde was giving that talk," Pippa said. "That was one of the things you were most excited for. How in the world did Carmen the Terrible get the gig?"

"Is this the chick you mentored, only to have her stab you in the back by taking your job?" Gilly asked.

"Yep, but in the grand scheme of life, she did me a favor—albeit her method could have been less crappy," I said. "Her taking my job gave me the push I needed to open Scents & Scentsability." And I regretted nothing. But it didn't stop my irritation at Carmen's apparent star status. It wasn't exactly that I wanted her to fail, but it didn't mean I wanted her success rubbed in my face.

"I'll text Barbara later to make sure she's okay. And honestly, I don't care if Carmen is the keynote speaker." I was a liar, liar, pants on fire, but whatever. There was no sense in letting Gilly and Pippa know that I was just the tiniest bit jealous of my old counterpart. I pulled my shoulders back and waved my hand dismissively. "I've got my girls, my man, and my health. I'm not going to let anything or anyone spoil our weekend."

Gilly lightly punched my upper arm. "That's the spirit."

"I had to work for that woman after you went on hiatus," Pippa said with a bitter expression on her lovely face. "I'm not sure I can be nice if I run into Queen Maleficent. She made me get her dry cleaning, Nora. Ugh."

"You got my dry cleaning for *me*," I pointed out.

Pippa furrowed her brow. "Because I wanted to, not because it was part of my job. Plus, you always said thank you."

I wasn't going to argue with her. Carmen had jumped at the chance to kick me when I was down by taking my job while my mother was sick. That alone had been enough to make Pippa, who was extremely loyal to me, dislike her on my behalf.

"You know Maleficent got a bad rap, don't you?" Gilly asked.

"What do you want me to call her? Disney Princess?" Pippa's lips thinned into a grimace. "Cruella De Vil, Queen of Hearts, Captain Hook?"

"Think of her as Voldemort." I nodded toward the front desk. "And let's avoid saying her name this weekend. We should get checked in. We'll deal with registration after we get our bags up to the room." We'd booked a double king suite for the three of us. Gilly and I had lost roshambo—best two out of three—to Pippa, so we got to share a bed, and Pippa got the other king all to herself.

"I'll handle the check-in," Pippa said. "You guys wait here with the bags." She took off before Gilly or I could object. Not that I would have. The line was long, and I didn't relish the idea of being crammed between a bunch of strangers.

"I'm going to get a drink." Gilly gestured at a table with lemon water and other beverages for conference guests. "Do you want anything?"

We'd driven for over two hours and had only stopped for a pee break once, so I declined with a shake of my head. "No, thanks."

She shrugged. "Suit yourself."

After Gilly left me, I heard a man say, "Well, I'll be, if it isn't Nora Black."

I looked behind me and saw a suave-looking man in an expensive tailored suit, his dark brown hair slightly gray at the temples, and his brown eyes crinkled at the corners. I hadn't seen him in a few years, but he hadn't changed much.

At least he was talking to me. The last time I'd seen him, nine years ago, I'd given him the "it's not you, it's me" breakup speech.

"Hello, Gregory," I said. "How are you?"

"Heart's all mended," he said, pressing his hands against his chest. "How are *you*?"

"Happy," I said simply. "Are you still with Selebrate?"

"I am. In fact, we're showing our new Stress-less meditation pods this weekend. You should come to our launch party tomorrow night. It's in the Rosewood Room on the sixth floor."

I'd read about the new meditation pods thanks to an article Gilly had texted me. They were supposed to be the second coming for finding peace and relaxation. And Gilly had been super excited about the Stress-less, in particular. She'd kill me if I tossed away an opportunity for her to stick her curvy butt in one. Even if it meant accepting an invite from my former boyfriend. "Sounds good, Gregory. Can I get a plus two?"

Gregory smiled. "You always did like to negotiate."

I laughed. "If I was negotiating, I would've said I had four friends, and bargained down to the two."

"Touché," he said. He nodded. "Any friend of yours is welcome. I'll add you and plus two to the list."

"Thanks." Gregory's invitation to the exclusive launch party brought back the zip of excitement I used to feel at these events. Although I hated to admit I missed anything from my old life.

"What about you?" he asked. "I heard you were out of the beauty business. Belliza really lost an asset when they let you go." He gave me a flirtatious smile. "Who are you with now?"

I smiled back, because a) Gregory was still a handsome man, and b) we'd been more than friends once, and c) I was flattered. "I opened a boutique shop back in my hometown."

He frowned. "Really. What are you selling?"

"Handmade lotions, soaps, face, and hair care items."

"Are you looking to expand? I have contacts in manufacturing that I could hook you up with. And," he added, "if you're looking for investors, I hope you'll call me."

I chuckled. "Not at this time. All my products are strictly organic, so they aren't long-term shelf-stable. Maybe sometime down the road."

"Got it. But let me know if you change your mind." He waved at a young brunette girl with her long straight hair pulled back into a chic ponytail. She was average height and model thin, wearing a cream-colored silk tank top and a pale pink pencil skirt, and a cross-body clutch bag a shade darker than her shirt. "That's my new assistant," he said. "Samantha Jones."

When Samantha approached, she wore rectangular-framed glasses and was clutching a pink tablet with a unicorn sticker on the back. I also noticed she wore the most expensive version of my own smartwatch, with a pearly pink band to match her pearly pink fingernails. I'd almost picked that one, but the only thing her watch did that mine didn't was show text messages and get email. Since I can't read words that small, even with my reading glasses, I hadn't thought it was worth the extra six hundred dollars.

"Samantha, this is Nora Black, an old friend of mine. Give her three guest invites for the launch party tomorrow night."

Samantha gave me a cordial nod. Her eyes jumped nervously. "I don't have the cards on me, but what's your room number? I'll have them sent up tonight."

"I don't have a room number, yet," I said. I glanced at Pippa, who had made it to the front of the line. "My friend is getting us checked in now."

Gregory pulled a business card from his pocket. "Do you at least have a pen?" he asked her impatiently.

"Yes, Mr. Paramount." She slid a pen out from the side of her clutch.

Gregory smiled at me as he wrote on the back of the card. He handed it to me. "Use this to get into the launch party tomorrow night."

He'd written, *Personal Guest of Gregory Paramount, so shut up and get this woman whatever she wants*.

I grinned as I took it and tucked it into my purse. "It's nice to see you again, Gregory."

"It's always nice to see you, Nora." He smiled and walked toward the registration tables.

Gilly came back over, holding a lemonade. "Who was that?" she whispered. "My gosh he's gorgeous!"

"Uh-huh," I agreed. "That was Gregory Paramount. He's the CEO of the Selebrate Corporation. They make beauty gadgets like tanning beds, zero-gravity chairs, and now, meditation pods, I suppose.

"Gregory Paramount," Gilly said as she tapped her chin. "I'd like to para-mount him. Can you introduce us?"

I gave her a sidelong look. "I thought you were off men."

"Only men in Garden Cove," she retorted.

"This is the first time you've been out of Garden Cove in years," I said.

"Exactly." She grinned and nudged me with her shoulder. "So...an introduction."

Pippa trotted back over, holding a bifold keycard holder. "Was that Gregory?"

"Yep. What room are we in?" I asked, trying to change the subject. Pippa was quite aware of my history with the man.

"You know him, too," Gilly said. "Can you introduce me? Nora doesn't seem to want to do the honors."

Pippa barked a laugh. "Maybe because Nora dated him for nearly four months about nine years ago."

Gilly turned on me, her brow raised. "Excuse me?"

"It wasn't a big deal," I said.

"He was in love with you, Nora. It doesn't get a much bigger deal than that."

I glared at Pippa. "We *both* realized it was a mistake."

"Yeah, because he was in love with you, and you told him, and I quote, *that's so nice of you to say.*"

I laughed. "It wasn't one of my finer moments. But I couldn't lie and tell him that I felt more than I did."

Gilly forced a smile, but I could see she was butt-hurt. "Why didn't you ever tell me?"

"Oh, Gils. You'd just gone through a messy divorce with Gio, and I liked Gregory, I really did, but please believe me when I say, there's nothing to tell. We only saw each other every other weekend for a few months because we both traveled for work." I shook my head. "He caught feelings, I didn't."

Gilly pursed her lips and wiggled them, then said, "So, BFF code means he's off the table, right?"

I knew she was teasing me, so I laughed. "Absolutely. You can't date someone I dated. I know we have that chiseled in stone somewhere and sealed with a blood pact."

Gilly crossed her arms over her chest and affected a pout. "You married Shawn after I dated him."

The Shawn she referred to was Shawn Rafferty, my ex-husband, the current chief of the Garden Cove Police, and my new boyfriend's boss.

"Really?" Pippa asked. "Do tell me more."

I rolled my eyes. "We were eleven years old, and it was not a date. It was spin-the-bottle at Mellie Chu's birthday party."

"Whatever happened to Mellie?" Gilly mused.

"She's a doctor over in Lampole," I reminded her.

"There you are, Gregory," a woman said enthusiastically and loudly enough for me to hear her over the dull roar of conversations happening in the lobby.

I looked over and saw Carmen Carraway, wearing a

deep red jumper with a plunging V-neck and a pair of red stilettos. I hadn't worn stilettos since my early forties, and my feet ached just looking at them.

Carmen was willowy and tall, like Pippa, only with bigger boobs, and the red complimented her dark hair and fair skin. She threw her arms around Gregory's neck and gave him a kiss, leaving a slight hint of redness from her lipstick on his mouth when they parted.

"Whoa," Gilly said. "Plot twist."

# CHAPTER 2

*P*ippa gasped. "He's dating Carmen."

"It looks like they're doing more than dating," Gilly said.

"They got engaged two weeks ago," announced a man who walked up next to us, his gaze on the couple.

Pippa squealed with delight. "Aaron!" She hugged the young man in his late twenties, dressed in a blue, slim-fit Italian suit with a white shirt, unbuttoned at the collar. He wore a stylish leather cross-body satchel big enough for a laptop and other items. "What are you doing here?"

"I'm Carmen's new *you*," he said with a pleasant smile. "I took over the position after you quit last April."

"Congratulations on the promotion, but I don't envy you. There's a reason I jumped at Nora's offer when she called. Carmen is demanding."

"You mean I'm not?" I asked. "I don't know if that's a compliment."

Pippa laughed. "Nora Black, meet Aaron Keller. Aaron

14

was an intern in the sales department. He came on a month after you took leave."

"The famous Nora Black." Aaron extended his hand.

I took his hand and gave it a shake. "More infamous than famous," I countered.

The young man chuckled. "Fair enough. What brings you guys here? I thought you were out of the beauty business."

"Not anymore," I said.

"Nora has a fantastic boutique shop in Garden Cove," Pippa said with enthusiasm. "She hand-makes almost all the products on our shelves."

"I used to vacation with my family in Garden Cove when I was a kid," Aaron said.

"So, two years ago," Pippa teased.

"Don't be such an ageist," he shot back with a grin.

I decided to intervene before Pippa told him to get off her lawn. "I grew up in Garden Cove, so starting a business there made sense."

Aaron smiled at me. "I'll tell my parents to stop by your shop the next time they go for a stay."

Pippa handed him a business card. "It's called Scents and Scentsability."

"Clever." He tucked it in his pocket. His gaze tracked to the registration table. "Uh-oh. I better go."

Aaron fast-walked toward his boss. Carmen was red-faced, her eyes wide with mild horror as Gregory faced off against a furious-looking woman.

"Holy crap," Gilly said. "That looks intense. Let's get closer so we can hear what's going on."

Pippa nodded and put her hand on my back as she and

Gilly steered me closer to the commotion. "We should probably go upstairs," I said without any real intent to walk away. I hated to admit it, but I wanted to know what was going on as much as they did. Even if it meant moving closer to *she who I said I wouldn't name*.

Unfortunately, we weren't the only nosy ones. A sizeable crowd of about twenty-plus conference attendees had gathered near the registration tables, and it wasn't for the welcome packets.

"This isn't the time or the place," Gregory told the woman. He didn't sound angry. More...weary. Like he'd dealt with her a lot.

She was short and curvy, with a champagne-blonde pixie-cut hairstyle, and wearing jeans and a t-shirt. And now that we were closer, I recognized her. "That's Remy Tarlington." She was older now, but who wasn't? And if looks could kill, Gregory would be dead.

"Who's Remy Tarlington?" Gilly asked.

"She's the head of product development for Selebrate. I met her when Gregory and I were going out. She and her wife barbequed for us once."

"Remy was fired from Selebrate shortly after you took your separation package from Belliza," Pippa said. "There was a big stink about it because Remy hired a lawyer to get the non-compete clause from her contract nulled since they let her go."

"Did she win?" I asked.

"I don't know." She shrugged. "It was still ongoing when I quit Belliza to come work for you."

Surprisingly, Aaron grabbed Remy by the upper arm. "You need to go," he said firmly. "Don't make a scene."

It was too late for that.

Remy's expression was a mixture of hurt and confusion as she stared at Carmen's assistant. "They won't get away with this," she said. "I won't let them." Remy turned a venomous gaze on Gregory. "Do you hear me? You won't get away with this!"

Aaron tried to lead her from the area, and she jerked hard away from him, careening in my direction.

"Watch out!" Gilly exclaimed as Remy collided with me, knocking us both to the cold tiled floor.

We stared at each other for a moment, her hazel-brown eyes glittering with tears. She looked angry and miserable, and she smelled like Meyer lemons.

*I see a woman with a blurred face because I never see the face in my visions. With her pixie haircut and curves that can be seen even under the bathrobe, I know it's Remy Tarlington. She's holding a cellphone to her ear. "I will get what I want from Paramount. He'll tell the world that he stole my design for the meditation pod, or I'll make him pay."*

*Alarm clangs through me, jarring my senses, as she pulls a micro 9mm from her robe pocket. I can't tell what brand it is, but it reminds me of the Sig Sauer my dad had bought my mom for an anniversary present one year. Remy taps the weapon against her thigh.*

*"Don't back out on your deal," she says. "You have as much to lose as I do. Don't forget it. Selebrate is making a lot of money off my hard work, and I'll be damned if they earn one more dime on my design."*

*She ended the call then sat down on a bed. "No, no," she mumbled. "I'll kill you before I let——"*

I snapped out of the vision as Remy Tarlington rolled

up to her feet. This time, Aaron managed to hustle her out of the hotel. Gilly and Pippa dragged me to a stand.

"Are you okay?" Gilly asked.

"Christ, Nora," Pippa said. "You're gonna break a hip."

"I'm fine," I said to Gilly, as I dusted off my butt. To Pippa, I added, "Quit treating me like I'm a hundred years old. My hips are intact, thank you very much."

She frowned and narrowed her gaze at me. "If you say so. Are you sure you're not hurt?"

"What do you want? For me to get a hula hoop?" I wiggled my hips to prove I could. I held back the fact that my wrist throbbed from reaching back to brace the landing. I could move it, and I would put ice on it when we got to the room. Even so, I didn't want anyone making a fuss over me here in the lobby of the hotel in front of a small crowd of people, including my ex-boyfriend and his fiancé, who happened to be my nemesis.

A nemesis who happened to be looking in my direction now. Craptastic.

"My God, Nora Black, as I live and breathe," Carmen said as she strode to me.

"Better than dying and not breathing," I muttered.

"What was that?" Carmen asked.

"I asked how you're doing," I said. I glanced down at the ginormous diamond in a platinum setting on her left ring finger. "Congratulations on the engagement."

Carmen waved her hand around nonchalantly. "Thank you." She glanced over her shoulder. "Oh, there's Donna Walker, the conference coordinator. I need to talk to her about my keynote address." She turned back to me. "Let's catch up over drinks this weekend."

"I'll have to check our schedule," I said with no intention of following through.

"Aw, and you still have Pippa around. That's so sweet." She jutted her lower lip in a slight pout. "It's nice to see you both together still, working your little store."

The "little" part didn't hurt, since Scents & Scentsability was a small shop. Still, it sounded as if Carmen was trying to insult me, and her condescending tone kind of steamed my buns. Even so, I was going to let it go because Carmen wasn't worth my ire.

Apparently, Gilly did not feel the same way.

"It *is* sweet," my BFF said. "Pippa was working for a complete shrew at her previous employment. The woman was a real witch in heels, if you get my drift. She jumped at the chance to quit and come work with Nora."

"Pippa had been working for me," Carmen said dryly. She arched a brow at Gilly. "I suppose I'm the witch."

"If the broom fits," Gilly replied.

"Okaaay," Pippa interrupted. She gripped Gilly's shoulders. "We should really get our bags up to the room."

"Good idea," I agreed. "So nice to see you, Carmen."

"You, too, Nora. I'm sure we'll run into each other again this weekend," Carmen said.

I waited until she was out of earshot to say, "Not if I see you first."

Gilly elbowed me. "Hah, I was going to say that."

I raised a brow at her. "If you were going to say it, you would have said it while she was still here."

My BFF snickered. "That's true."

"You two are awful," Pippa said with a grin. "One of the many reasons I love you both."

I kept an eye on Carmen as she crossed the room. A man in a pair of tan pants and a blue Henley shirt stopped her short, and they began to talk. The guy looked familiar, but I couldn't tell if it was because he had worked for Belliza or if it was because he'd been a client. I usually had an excellent memory for faces and names, so it irked me that his escaped me.

I was going to ask Pippa, but Aaron Keller rejoined us. "Hey, Pip." He seemed nonplussed about having to escort Remy Tarlington from the hotel. "Can I help you ladies with your bags?"

"Is the Queen of Mean paying you so little you've taken an extra job as a bellhop?" Pippa asked.

"Carmen pays me just fine. Besides, I'm getting a promotion soon." He blinked, a slow grin turning up his lips. "I thought you might want some help."

Pippa laughed. "I think we can manage, but thanks, Aaron."

"Maybe we can get some lunch or, better yet, dinner?"

"Are you flirting with me?"

"Only if you want to be flirted with."

"I have a boyfriend."

He smirked. "You deserve a man friend."

Pippa's mouth dropped open as her eyes widened with incredulity.

I, being the supportive friend I am, snorted a laugh. "Yeah, Pip, you need a man friend."

"Jordy is plenty man," she defended.

"Oh, really," Gilly interjected. "Do tell us more?"

I laughed again.

Aaron didn't seem too dejected. He winked at Pippa. "If you change your mind, I'll be around."

The three of us watched with a fair amount of awe as he walked away.

"Wowza." Gilly shook her hand as if she'd touched something hot. "That boy has *cajones* for days."

"Boxes?" Pippa asked.

I giggled. "You know she meant *cojones*."

"Balls," Gilly said. "I mean balls."

"We know," Pippa and I said together. We high-fived.

Then the three of us laughed.

Gilly put an arm over each of our shoulders. "This is going to be the best girls' weekend ever."

"Hell, yeah," Pippa agreed. "The best."

"This was such a great idea," I added enthusiastically. However, I couldn't stop thinking about my vision of Remy Tarlington holding a gun and threatening to kill someone.

# CHAPTER 3

*T*he bathroom in the suite was large, with the actual toilet having its own little room space separate from the shower. That would come in handy with my post-hysterectomy bladder. I hadn't shared a hotel room with anyone since I was a struggling intern for Belliza Beauty. Still, I was looking forward to spending quality time with two of my favorite people.

"Gilly, you've got enough product here to cover all fifty-one contestants in the Miss Beautiful United States Pageant," Pippa complained.

"Why are there fifty-one?" Gilly asked, unperturbed. "We only have fifty states."

"Washington, D.C." I ignored the ache in my wrist and my tailbone. It wasn't too bad, yet, but I would need to get some ice on it soon if I wanted to enjoy the rest of our trip. "It has a pageant contestant, but it's not a state."

"Not yet." Gilly looked down at her array of makeup, skincare, and hair care products. She'd given up on going gray after a month when an inch of white fluff sprouted from the crown of her head. It was hard to hide, even with highlights. However, she had gone with a dark honey-blonde to replace the chestnut brown, and it was seriously flattering with her light brown eyes. "You guys have plenty of room up here for your stuff. And I'm happy to share any of my makeup or whatever with you."

I grabbed a melon lip gloss from her tray. "This looks pretty."

"The color would be so good on you," Gilly said.

Pippa nodded. "It really would." She crossed her arms over her chest. "Now, are we going to talk about what happened with your ex and that woman Remy? Because that was some nasty business."

"I agree." In the vision I'd had, Remy had sounded desperate. And that threat...was she actually prepared to kill someone, or had it been an idle threat? I couldn't shake the feeling that something terrible was about to happen. Since I didn't see the future in my visions, there was no way for me to be certain. I rubbed my sore wrist. "I got a scent memory when Remy fell on me."

"One of your smell-o-visions?" Gilly's eyebrows shot up. "Why didn't you tell us?"

"I'm telling you now." I walked out into the room and unzipped my suitcase. "It freaked me out."

"Spill it," Gilly said.

"Remy was on the phone with someone, and she was ranting about how Gregory had stolen some design from her for a meditation pod." I hung up my flapper dress in the closet. "She had a gun."

"A gun?" Pippa's alarm matched my own. "Do you

23

think she was talking about Selebrate's new Stress-less meditation pod? Do you think Gregory would do that?"

I shook my head. "I don't know. I mean, it doesn't sound like him. He always liked Remy. They were friends. Or at least, they used to be."

"People change," Gilly said.

"Or sometimes they just show you who they really are," I replied dryly.

"Lord, Nora. That's jaded even for you." Gilly gave me a disappointed frown. "We've all changed. And thank heavens, right?"

I smiled sheepishly. "I guess if you can move on from neon spandex mini-dresses, then anyone can change."

"Nora Black!" Her eyes widened, and she smacked me in the arm. "It was the early nineties. Besides, I made those dresses look good."

"Yeah, you did." I nudged her. "Damn good. I knew how to rock padded shoulders and ripped jeans."

Gilly let out a girlish squeal. "Oh my gosh, remember those high-waisted jeans that were so tight we had to lay on the bed to zip them up with pliers?"

"Or wire hangers." I cringed. "I don't miss skintight high-waisted jeans."

"They are back in fashion," Gilly said. "Along with ripped jeans."

"Everything old is new again."

"Except for my neck." Gilly smoothed her hand under her chin down her neck. "But totally."

We both smiled as we reminisced about our youth.

"In the early nineties, I was in elementary school," Pippa said, bringing both Gilly and me back to reality.

"Can we get unpacked so we can go get registered? Besides, there's a welcome brunch happening right now, and I'm peckish."

"You know how to kill a vibe," Gilly said on a laugh.

Pippa smirked. "Is that what we were doing? Vibing?"

"Oh, to be so young." I gave her chin a gentle pinch. "And so impatient."

"You mean like that Aaron guy?" Gilly grinned at Pippa. "He seems really impatient about getting into your pants."

Pippa laughed. "The only guy getting into my pants is back in Garden Cove, making lattes."

Our single friend sighed. "I don't blame you. Jordy's a catch. Honest, hardworking, and super easy on the eyes."

"You'll find the right someone," I told her.

"I'm not sure I want to," she said. "At least not for a year or two. The kids have another year of school, and after what happened with Lloyd—"

"Gilly Martin," Pippa chided. "What happened with Lloyd was not your fault."

"No. You're right. But even if someone hadn't killed him and I hadn't been blamed for it, the man was toxic. He got physical with me. He showed up at Nora's spoiling for a fight, and then he took out a restraining order against her. Things would have continued to get a whole lot worse if he hadn't died. I'd like to say there were signs, but the truth is, I didn't see any. So, I think I am going to lay off men for a while, at least until Marco and Ari are safely off to college."

I gave Gilly a quick hug. "You're too hard on yourself."

"Maybe, but I'm due for some tough love, even if it has to come from me." She wiped at her eyes.

"Stop," I said softly. "Or you're going to make me cry with you."

Pippa clapped her hands then rubbed them together. "Come on now. We're here to celebrate Nora's birthday and have a good time."

"Epic," Gilly agreed. "We're going to make this birthday the best ever."

Last year for my birthday, I'd been eyeball deep in grief. My mother had died a few months before I turned fifty-one. My chest squeezed as I pictured her on my fiftieth birthday. The cancer hadn't ravaged her yet, and I remembered the way she'd laughed when I'd blown out the trick candle she'd put on my cake when it relit.

I swallowed the knot in my throat. "Best birthday," I said.

Both of them looked at me like I was a fragile egg ready to crack if they didn't handle me with care. "I'm fine," I added more robustly. "Isn't there some registering and snacking to do?"

Gilly nodded. "We better hurry before Pippa gets any thinner," she said. "She might blow away."

Pippa arched her brow. "As long as you aren't planning on blowing out Nora's candles, I think I'm safe."

"Ouch," I said, shrugging off the melancholy. I shook my fingers as if I'd touched a hot stove. "Serious burn."

"That's what the fire department said," Gilly joked. She and Pippa laughed.

"You're almost as old as I am, Gils," I reminded her.

Gilly, who'd finished unpacking both her suitcases

during our exchange, stripped off her tank top. She pulled on a light, stretch-knit yellow blouse that dressed up her khaki chinos. "I'm four months younger, thank you very much."

I stuck my tongue out at her.

"Very mature," she said, sticking out her tongue as she kicked off her sandals and put on a pair of pale yellow open-toed shooties. She checked out her butt in the mirror. "How do I look?"

"You're adorable, and you know it," I said.

"Agreed," said Pippa. She'd changed into a gauzy maroon blouse with a black camisole under but kept on the same shoes and pants. "Are we ready?"

I wanted to ice my sore bits, but not in front of the two mother hens in my life.

"Why don't you two go ahead? I'm just going to put up my feet for a minute. I'll meet you downstairs."

"Are you feeling okay?" Gilly asked. "I have ibuprofen in my purse if you want some."

I smiled. "I'm fine. Honest. I want to decompress. You know how I am."

Pippa cast me a knowing look. She'd been my sidekick too long not to recognize when I needed a minute. "If you decide you want us to bring you back some snacks, text me," she said.

"Maybe they'll have eggplant and tacos," Gilly teased.

I, once again, regretted telling her about my failed attempts to sext with Ezra. But I wasn't one to pass up tacos. "If they have any street tacos, definitely grab some for me."

After they left, I took off my makeup and got into a

pair of loose yoga pants. I planned to take a short nap, so I wanted to be comfortable. After, I slipped on my flip-flops, grabbed the room key and an ice bucket, then headed down the hall to the ice maker. A loudly whirring cola machine had been squeezed in next to the ice. The price was two dollars and fifty cents per bottle, and it took credit cards. Ugh. I remembered when you could get a Coke for three quarters. Luckily, Gilly had packed some Diet Cokes in her shoe suitcase. Smart girl.

I put the bucket under the nozzle and pressed the button. Shaved ice, the good kind that you get at the convenience store, spit out into the bucket. Yay! It would be easier on the tush and really excellent in a cup of Diet Coke.

I heard the rumblings of conversation coming from the hallway. I recognized Gregory's voice right away. I stayed in the ice room because, while I wasn't interested in Gregory anymore, I was vain enough that I didn't want him to see me in no makeup, yoga pants, and flip-flops. I felt as frozen as the shaved ice in the bucket I held.

"What do you mean there's a problem, Samantha?" Gregory asked.

"The pod sparked when we plugged it in, and the halo is malfunctioning," his assistant said. "I've left Carl three voicemails. He hasn't yet returned my calls."

"This is a disaster. It's the only prototype we have."

"It was working just fine last night when Carl tested it. I think someone tampered with it," she whispered harshly. "We can't demonstrate the pod if it's broken. It could kill someone."

"Damn it," Gregory said. "This is Brian Langford's

doing," he seethed. "That bastard. I'll kill him. Did you talk to security?"

"Of course," she told him. "They're gathering footage from the hall outside the room and the elevator, but there were a lot of people in both areas. The security guy said it might be hard to see someone going into the room."

"Tell Robson I want to review the security tapes from last night, from when our team finished the setup until the time you discovered the sabotage. I have my suspicions, and if I see that no-good son-of-a-bitch, I will see him in jail for this."

"Yes, Mr. Paramount," Samantha said. "Should we cancel the event?"

"Christ, no, Samantha. Forget Carl. Call Development and have them send someone else from the design team over here pronto and get the damned pod fixed in time for our showcase tomorrow night. Cancel the event?" He scoffed. "Do you know how much money I've invested in this launch?"

I eased forward enough to peek out from behind the wall of the alcove.

The lines in Gregory's forehead had turned into canyons of stress, and Samantha's pinched expression revealed panic and worry. She gripped her pink tablet as if it were a security blanket.

"If someone can't fix this mess, Sam," said Gregory as he met her gaze, "then *someone* will be looking for another job."

*Yikes.* I ducked back into the ice room. I didn't remember Gregory being so harsh. Then again, we only dated for a few months. That was barely enough time to figure out favorite foods and songs, much less stress reactions and temperaments.

I heard the chiming tones of a cellphone ringing. Then Gregory said, "I have to take this." I heard him whispering, his voice growing distant as he walked away.

I peeked around the corner again and saw Samantha holding her phone. She punched a button on the screen then she readjusted the Bluetooth receiver in her ear. Dang it. I was not going to casually stroll into the hallway now. She'd know that I'd overheard everything. I returned to my hiding spot.

"You need to take care of this," I heard Samantha say. "I don't care," she said, her tone edged with panic. "Please. It's getting out of hand."

*What's getting out of hand?*

The ice machine motor kicked in, making a loud grinding sound. The scents of gear oil and electrical exhaust filled the space.

*"Oh, God, yes," a man says with a groan. I can't see his face, or the woman he's with for that matter, but his pants are down, and her dress is up, and...ahem, things are culminating to a climax.*

*There are several more seconds of gawd-awful noises from the couple.*

*Cripes. As often as I'd wished I could see faces in my visions, this was the first time I wished other body parts could be blurred.*

"Oh, hell, no." Samantha be damned. I stumbled into the hallway as the lustful vision faded. Luckily, Gregory's assistant was gone. I hurried down the hall and into the suite, wishing there really was such a thing as brain bleach.

I walked into the bathroom and put the ice bucket on the counter. I couldn't get Samantha's panicked words out of my head. *We can't demonstrate the pod if it's broken. It could kill someone.* She'd thought the machine had been tampered with? But by whom? This Brian Langford person? And who or what did Samantha want to take care of? Remy Tarlington? Maybe. In the vision, Remy had said that Selebrate, and Gregory in particular, had stolen her designs for a pod.

So far, only one thing was certain. This spa weekend was starting to feel anything but relaxing.

*a*n hour later, me and my frozen body parts were on the elevator with eight other people heading to the first-floor lobby. I wore my vee-neck floral summer dress that looked super cute, but also high end. I'd bought it, along with a few other choice items, just for this trip. I wasn't sure who I was trying to impress, but the new clothes made me feel good, and maybe that was all that mattered.

Gilly had texted me that she and Pippa were on the third floor for the vendor tables, and then they were heading to the meet and greet in the Walnut Room. She took great care to let me know that she'd scoped out the food situation, and they had no tacos...or eggplants. I'd giggled because I'd just got done texting with Ezra to let him know we'd arrived safe and sound, and he'd texted me back with a few choice emojis.

Thinking about the text made me smile.

"Are you here for the convention?" a young woman, not more than twenty-five, asked.

"I am," I answered politely. "Just on my way to register now."

She was about an inch taller than me, but on the heavy side. Her blonde bob had chunky layers of pink and purple streaks, and her eyes were so light blue, I wondered if she was wearing colored contacts. The lanyard hanging around her neck had a convention name badge hanging from it that said, Blanche Michaels. Above her name was the title Guest Relations.

"You look familiar," she said. "Are you an influencer?"

I choked back a laugh at the idea. "Hardly."

"No." She shook her head. "I know I know you. Do you make artisan luxury soaps?"

"I do." I couldn't hide my astonishment. Maybe I wasn't the only psychic in this hotel. "How could you know that?"

Her eyes widened. "You're Nora Black," she said. "I've been following your videos on CraftTube. Are you one of the guest speakers? I'd love to see a live demonstration."

"Wow. Uhm, no. I'm really just here to celebrate my birthday with my friends, and to check out what's new in the beauty world. But thanks for the vote of confidence." Pippa had made a few videos of me demonstrating how to make different kinds of soaps. Nonetheless, our channel had less than a thousand subscribers. "You must be the one person who watches."

Her cherubic face lit up with excitement. "Are you kidding me? I have to thank you. I've made the basil lemon soap, the eucalyptus lavender, and the ocean loaf that looks like a sandy beach when you slice through it. You are amazing."

I blushed as a few people in the elevator started paying attention to our conversation. I'd been pretty proud of the ocean loaf, and the soap had been a popular seller, especially with so many people doing beachy themes in their guest bathrooms. "Uhm, thanks. That's so nice to hear."

Blanche took it upon herself to announce to the small audience of five women and two men in the elevator with us that, "This is Nora Black. She has a Scents and Scentsability channel on CraftTube. You have to check her out."

There were a few polite murmurs and head nods. I was grinning now, feeling a mixture of embarrassment and pride.

"When are you coming out with your next series?" she asked.

"Series?"

"You know, lotions, maybe? Or some of those body washes I've seen on your shop's website. You know there is a handcrafted component to the convention. You should totally apply to be a guest demonstrator next year." She shook her head. "I'm being pushy. I'm so sorry. I really am thrilled to meet you, Ms. Black."

"It's nice to meet you, too, Blanche."

The woman went up on her toes, body language equivalent of a squeal of delight. "If you need anything this weekend, you come find me. I'll get you taken care of."

"That's so nice of you." Her adoration was sweet, but I'll admit it made me uncomfortable. Much to my relief, the elevator doors opened. I gave Blanche a smile. "You take care now."

When I was out in the lobby, I couldn't believe how many people were crowded into the space. There had to be at least a hundred convention-goers lined up for registration. Damn it. I should have come down earlier with my friends. I'm not tall. By Pippa and Gilly's standards, I'm downright short, and I hated standing in a line where I couldn't see over or around anyone in front of me. My scent-ability was getting a workout, too. All the glimpses of memories related to the cologne and perfume wafting in the stifling air made me dizzy. If the lines didn't move faster, I would have to sit down and wait until the crowd thinned.

Someone tapped my shoulder. I glanced over and saw Blanche with a conspiratorial smile on her face. She leaned in and whispered, "Come with me."

I'm a fan of the *Terminator* franchise, so mentally, I added, "If you want to live." Only, I wasn't Sarah Connor, and Blanche was not a cyborg sent from the future to save me.

"I'll lose my place in line," I said in the same hushed tone without any real conviction. I did not want to be in this place with all these people anymore.

"Trust me," she said.

So, I did. Blanche threaded us through the milling convention-goers like an expert seamstress. She took me around the corner to a staff-only area behind the registration tables.

"Here you go," she said, picking up a bag from against the wall and handing it to me. "All of your convention stuff is inside."

That's when I realized Blanche had done me a legiti-

35

mate solid and completed my registration for me. "Oh my gosh, Blanche. Thank you so much."

Her face lit up again. "Are you kidding? It's my pleasure." A hint of a smile formed on her lips. "I've upgraded your registration to VIP. It will get you into all the events."

"That's amazing."

She grinned. "Happy birthday, Ms. Black. And can I just say, your skin is incredible. You should definitely do a video on your skincare routines."

Okay, Blanche was becoming one of my favorite people. "I might just do that," I told her. I gave her a quick hug. "And, please, call me Nora. Are you sure you won't get in trouble for this?" I pointed to the VIP badge.

"We always have extras that some of the more significant sponsors pay for that never get used.

I raised a brow. "How many extras?"

"At least a couple dozen." She beamed a smile at me. "How many do you need?"

"Two more. I'm here with two of my best girlfriends. I completely understand if you can't, though, so no pressure."

"It's my pleasure. I put my business card with my personal cell number in your registration packet. Call me after four. I'll have two VIP badges ready for you."

"I'll do that. You are the best, Blanche." I dug through the bag as I walked back to the elevators and grabbed my lanyard with my name badge. Above my name was a gold VIP sticker. I grinned to myself as I hung it around my neck. I couldn't wait to tell Pippa and Gilly about my newfound celebrity status.

People were queued up for the elevator. Crowds fueled the energy of conventions. But with my ability to read people's scent memories, the shoulder-to-shoulder bustles had become like cable TV and streaming apps. In other words, so much to watch, but nothing I wanted to see.

As the elevators filled up and doors closed, I inched forward. I pulled out my phone to play Angry Word Jumble. Gilly's daughter Ari had put the app on my phone, and I found the game amusing and diverting.

Then I heard Carmen's voice.

No. Ugh. I ducked my head. If I was lucky, she wouldn't see me in the sea of bodies. I didn't hate her for taking my job. I mean, not really. While Carmen and I hadn't been besties, we'd had the makings of a real friendship before I'd taken a leave of absence to take care of Mom. The way Carmen had accepted my job before I'd even been offered early retirement by the company had felt like a stab in the back.

Between my mother's death and the loss of the job I'd held for seventeen years, I'd been filled with every kind of grief. But in the end, I was happy to be free of Belliza Beauty. I might have missed the hustle. *A little.* However, I truly loved my new life in Garden Cove.

"I'll need you to set up the new Biologenesis display," Carmen said. "Yes, in the Oak Room. How am I supposed to know how many outlets the room has? Ask someone. Okay. Yes. It's right next to Rosewood on the sixth floor. Thank you."

I wasn't looking at her, but since no one within earshot was answering her, I figured she was talking on the phone. I wasn't familiar with Biologenesis. Was that a new line of skincare for Belliza? Biogenesis was a reproduction of cells or something along those lines. Most skincare routines that promised cell rejuvenation couldn't deliver, but still, my interest was piqued.

The elevator door opened again. I shuffled in behind three others, a middle-aged woman, and a young couple engaged in handholding and neck-nuzzling. I moved to the opposite side of them, in case one of them was wearing a bedroom scent. I'd already had one X-rated vision today, and I wasn't looking for another. Unfortunately, Carmen got on the elevator before the doors closed. Our eyes met.

*Well, crap.* I smiled. "Hey, fancy meeting you here."

Carmen chuckled. "Small world." She moved in close to me as the last two people entered. "Three, please," she said to a man who was standing near the buttons. "What floor, Nora?"

"Same," I said. "I'm joining my friends at the meet and greet."

"Nice." She glanced at my badge. "You should check out the champagne brunch Belliza is sponsoring. It's in the Oak Room for VIPs."

"I'm not actually..." I stop just short of admitting the truth. I didn't care what Carmen thought of me, but I didn't want to put Blanche's job in jeopardy. "Uhm, maybe."

She smiled, her gaze pivoting to my body and back to my face. "All the snacks are low carb," she said with enthusiasm.

"It's good you have champagne to wash them down then." I smiled even harder.

Carmen blinked as she took in my words, her perfect lips bowing into a frown.

The elevator stopped on the third floor, and the doors opened. I was clutching my phone so hard my fingers hurt.

Carmen went ahead of me, and I followed her out because the only other choice was to ride the elevator again. She went left, so I went right. Because I wanted to put as much distance between Carmen and myself as possible. If Carmen was New York, I wanted to be Alaska. Or Hawaii. Even better. There would be an ocean between us.

Gilly had said she and Pippa were in the Walnut room, so I followed the corridor until I saw a blurry "W" in a word on a door. I stopped short of pushing my way inside when I heard two men arguing.

"You've been stealing from us for years. Including the idea for a zone meditation pod," one of the men said. "Don't act like the victim, Paramount."

"You've plagiarized our marketing, you stole my design plans, and now you've sabotaged the pod, Langford," the other, who was definitely Gregory, snarled. "When I find proof, I will ruin you."

"You've got a lot of nerve. We've been developing our Zensation meditation pod long before you came up with the Stress-less. And Tarlington came to me after you threw her away."

Remy Tarlington had accused Selebrate of stealing her designs. Had she given this Langford guy the plans in retaliation? Was she guilty of industrial espionage? If she was, she was damn lucky she only got fired and not thrown in jail. I knew I should stop listening, but this was the kind of intrigue that I lived for, and I couldn't make myself walk away.

"Frankly, you're an idiot," Langford continued. "You rushed the pod to market just to try and beat us. If there's been any sabotage, it's your own."

The man barreled around the corner and almost knocked me over. I yipped and hugged the wall to avoid another fall. He was the tan pants-blue Henley guy who had been talking to Carmen earlier in the lobby. I didn't recognize the name Brian Langford, but I swore I knew the guy from somewhere.

Interesting.

"Nora?" Gregory said with some surprise as he came around the corner. His face was flushed. "Are you looking for me?"

I pointed to the door. "I'm going into the Walnut Room for the meet and greet."

"That's the Willow Room."

"Oh. I don't have my glasses on." It sounded like a lame excuse, but the truth was I couldn't see up close very well without them. I was officially farsighted, but still too vain to wear glasses all the time.

The crease between his eyes deepened. He shook his head and gave me a tight smile. "I can walk you down if you want."

"Sure. Thanks." I resisted the urge to put my hand on his arm when I asked, "Is everything okay?"

"Why do you ask?"

"I couldn't help but overhear the end of your conversation with your friend. It was pretty intense."

"Brian Langford isn't a friend." He grimaced. "I don't want to talk about him."

"Okay," I said. "None of my business."

"There's the Walnut Room," Gregory said. There were dozens of people milling in and out of the place. Duh.

I jerked my thumb toward them. "Well, I better get in there before they run out of food and drinks."

I couldn't get Langford's accusation out of my mind that Remy had gone to them. Had she betrayed Gregory? The vision I'd had from her suggested it wasn't the case. Was stealing her own designs still industrial espionage?

*"I will get what I want from Paramount. He'll tell the world that he stole my design for the meditation pod, or I'll make him pay,"* she had said. Had she been talking to Langford?

Had she gone to Langford's company after she'd been fired?

Was that one of the ways she intended to make him pay, by giving company secrets to the enemy? I sighed. This wasn't my business, I reminded myself. I saw Gilly and Pippa in the corner of the room, waving at me.

My only business this weekend was to have fun, not stick my psychic smell-o-vision where it didn't belong.

CHAPTER 5

The Walnut Room was an ample venue space, and there were tables of canapes and iced drinks—non-alcoholic, of course—along the walls. In the middle of the area were numerous tall tables meant for people to stand at and eat. No chairs to be seen, though. Gilly had gone over to grab enough sustenance to get us through the afternoon, but not so much as to spoil our dinner at Darbie's, a Michelin-starred restaurant. It had been part of my birthday request to eat there, and we'd been lucky to get the reservation. I was grateful to be in a corner with Pippa, who nabbed the one table far away from the sheer number of bodies milling around.

"Did you pay to upgrade to a Gold Pass?" Pippa asked, slightly incredulous.

"Not hardly." I snorted. I mean, I wasn't miserly, but we'd already spent around a thousand dollars for the three of us to attend, not including the hotel room or the car rental. No way was I spending another three thousand to get special access to exclusive events and a few extra meals. Scent & Scentsability didn't need the latest and greatest in beauty aids. Besides, I was here to destress, not to schmooze.

"You know this is your doing, Pip," I said. "It turns out that the one person watching those demonstration videos you published on CraftTube works for the convention in guest relations. Her name is Blanche. She surprised me with this." I held up the badge. "And," I did a drum roll with my fingers on the tabletop, "I got you and Gilly VIP badges as well. I'm supposed to call her after four this afternoon to pick them up."

Pippa clapped her hands. "I told you CraftTube was a good idea! Look how it's paying off in dividends."

"You're brilliant." My stomach rumbled. "Do you see Gilly? I'm starved."

Since Pippa was taller, she was usually the designated lookout. "There." She pointed into the crowd. "It looks like she's getting some puff pastries."

The culinary spread in the Walnut Room was definitely not low carb.

"Oh, she's coming back now. And damn, she's got three plates."

Gilly had worked as a waitress when she was in high school, and the way she balanced those plates bordered on professional. She put them down, along with a stack of napkins. She'd created a dish of vegetable-esque appetizers, another for a variety of savory pastries, and the last stacked with tiny desserts.

I grabbed one from the veggie plate that looked like it had melon wrapped in prosciutto. I popped it into my mouth and then spit it out in one of the napkins. "That's not prosciutto."

"It's thin-sliced smoked salmon wrapped around white cheddar. It's delicious." Gilly ate one to punctuate her point. Her face squinched. "So good," she said, looking like she wanted to spit it out as well.

"What else have you got?" I went with a safer choice —bruschetta with tomato, fresh chopped basil, pesto, and mozzarella. I took a bite, but I think cardboard had more flavor. I swallowed it reluctantly. "How can anyone mess up bruschetta?"

Gilly gave me a bland stare. "It's free, Nora. What do you want?"

Pippa made a face when she sniffed what looked like a crab roll. "I'd prefer something that didn't give me salmonella."

I laughed. "Same." Then I thought about the Belliza Brunch. Carmen had told me about it, but it wasn't like she'd be there, right? At least not the whole time. And while the "low carb" dig had felt personal, some of my favorite foods were low carb. Like bacon and cheese. "I know where we can get some decent food and champagne. Are you in?"

"You had me at decent food," Pippa said.

"What kind of champagne?" Gilly asked. "Because I don't want anything that comes in a box."

I laughed again. "Oh, stop. Like you said, it's free, right?" I personally thought all champagne tasted funky. Gilly was the connoisseur in our group. A side effect of being married to a world-class chef who took wine seriously. "My old company is hosting it, so it should be good."

Pippa, who hadn't said a word during this exchange, crossed her arms over her chest and pursed her lips at me. "Are we really not going to discuss Gregory? We saw you talking to him just outside the door."

Gilly's brows shot up. "Spill."

I rolled my eyes. "Remember I told you guys about the vision I'd had when Remy fell on me?"

"Yes, she had a gun and was threatening to kill someone," Gilly answered.

"Not exactly, but sort of, I guess. But Remy also said she'd make Gregory pay for whatever she thinks he did."

Pippa nodded.

"Well, when I was coming here, I took off the wrong way out of the elevator and ended up outside the Willow Room instead of the Walnut Room."

Gilly gave me a disapproving head shake. "This is why you need to keep your reading glasses on you at all times."

"Thank you for those wonderful words of wisdom. I will cherish them always." I flashed her a syrupy smile. "Should I continue, or do you want me to go up to the room to get my glasses first?"

She mirrored my smile. "I'm always glad to impart sage advice for a friend. Like taking ginkgo so you'll stop forgetting to take your glasses with you. However, at this moment in time, you should definitely continue."

"Are you certain?" I asked. "Because I'll happily—"

"Oh, for heaven's sake, Nora." Pippa narrowed her gaze at both of us and made a hurry-up gesture with her hand. "Just get on with it. What did Gregory want?"

"He..." Crap. I blinked as I tried to remember what I

was saying. Every once in a while, I get what I like to call brain zaps. "Where did I leave off?"

"You walked to the Willow Room because you didn't have your glasses," Pippa said. She glared at Gilly, daring her to say anything.

Gilly raised her brow, then put the imaginary key into the imaginary lock on her lips and gave it a twist.

"That's right. The Willow Room. So, I'm standing out in front of the room, and I hear two men arguing."

"And?" Gilly asked.

"Did your invisible lock break?" I asked.

"It's defective," she quipped. "I'm going to return it for a refund."

Pippa, with no small amount of exasperation, said, "I'm going to return both of you if you don't stop getting off-topic."

"You're stuck with us." I gave her a nudge. "There is a strict no-return policy when it comes to our friendship."

"And there are definitely no refunds," Gilly added. "That check has been spent."

"No one pays by check anymore," Pippa said.

"Roger, the water guy, insists on a check," I disagreed. "I keep a checkbook just for him. Well, him and the DMV."

Pippa made small circles in the air with her thin fingers. "So, you're outside the Willow Room, and you hear an argument. Keep going."

"That's right. Gregory was arguing with Brian Langford."

"Brian Langford is a VP of development over at Konash Technologies. They make stuff for aestheticians like lasers for hair removal and phototherapy gadgets for collagen rejuvenation," Pippa said.

"I have a Konash steamer in the second massage room for when I do facials. They make good products," Gilly added.

"Well, it seems he's gotten into the meditation pod business as well," I said. "Gregory accused him of stealing marketing, designs, and such from him. And he accused Langford of damaging the Stress-less pod."

"Those are some strong allegations," Pippa said.

"I know, right? Oh! Cripes. I can't believe I left this out. After you all left the room, I went to get ice. While I was in the ice machine room, I overheard Gregory and his assistant talking about the new meditation pod he's launching tomorrow night. It's been sabotaged. At first, I thought Remy might have messed with the machine, but now, who knows."

Gilly gasped just as she took another bite of the yucky bruschetta and began to cough.

Pippa patted her back. "Do you think it has anything to do with the incident with Remy? You said you heard her talking about them stealing her design."

I nodded. "Possibly. Langford had said that Remy went to him."

"With what?" Pippa asked. If she had been sitting down, she would have been on the edge of her seat.

"I'm assuming the pod, but I don't know. Langford's company is launching a pod called Zensation that's in direct competition with the Stress-less."

"I love that name," Pippa said. "Though Stress-less is good, too."

Gilly, who'd finally stopped coughing, asked, "Anything else you want to tell us?"

"Nope. That's it." I skipped the part about the couple having sex near the ice maker. Because *ew*. "Anyway. Gregory saw me after the argument was over and offered to walk me here."

"Is that how you got the VIP badge?" Gilly asked. "Gregory gave it to you because he...what, was trying to buy your silence?"

I touched the lanyard. "There's nothing I could tell. Not really. And the badge is a gift from a fan."

"Yeah, it is." Pippa grinned. "CraftTube is paying off big time."

"Big time is a stretch, but yes. I suppose so. A nice girl named Blanche likes to watch my soap-making demonstrations. She gave me the upgrade for my birthday. And she is arranging for upgrades for you two."

Gilly grinned. "I am about to lose my cool and do a friggin' touchdown dance. I wanted to go to the Londa Angelista VIP Room so badly, I was thinking about trying to sneak in. I heard they have the swankiest swag."

"Let's do it," I said. "But not now. Right now, I want some decent food."

"Do you think they'll let us in without already having the VIP badge?" Pippa asked.

"We won't know unless we try. Right?"

"If we can't get in," Pippa replied. "You grab us some food, and we'll take it up to the room. We can drink a little mini-bar wine, relax on the balcony, and give our Zen a head start."

A tension knot had formed in my neck just since our

arrival. I stretched to loosen it up. "I'm onboard," I said. "Let the unwinding begin."

# CHAPTER 6

*T*he Oak Room was on the sixth floor, and unlike the crowded, high-energy meet and greet, the mood here was more reserved.

I flashed my badge at a security guy named Raul, who stood watch over the door.

"You can go in," he said. "But I'm afraid your friends will have to wait out here."

"I was told I could bring guests," I lied. "Besides, they have VIP badges coming."

Raul crossed his beefy arms across his chest and shook his head. "When they get them, they can go in with you. Until then, I have strict orders."

Holy cow, security was tight for the Gold events.

"I'd like to talk to your supervisor," Gilly said in a display of indignation that made me snarf.

Raul also looked amused. He jerked his thumb toward a dark-haired man in a blue suit jacket and black dress pants talking to another guy who looked like he spent way too much time in the gym. "There's my boss. Feel free to go have a chat."

His boss happened to look up at that moment, and he excused himself from the muscle head and crossed the corridor to us. He had several gadget pouches on his belt, including a radio, phone, and handcuffs. He wore a hotel badge over his left breast pocket that identified him as Luke Robson, Hotel Security.

"Is there a problem here?" he asked. He had an imposing presence, like someone used to being in charge.

"No problem," I said.

"These three want to go inside, but only one has a VIP pass," Raul said.

I cast him a look that I hoped said, "Really, Raul?"

He shrugged. The corner of his mouth ticked up in a smirk.

Gilly stepped up. "It's our friend's birthday." She pointed at me. "Couldn't you just make a teeny-weenie exception?"

"I'm sorry, ladies, but you'll have to wait outside for the birthday girl. Only gold badges." Robson glanced over his shoulder. "I'm truly sorry. If it were up to me, I'd let you guys in."

"Okay," I said.

Gilly, unperturbed, looked at Robson. "How long until this shindig shuts down?"

His brow went up. "It's over at three o'clock."

She beamed her most Gilly smile at him, and I could see that Luke Robson wasn't immune to her charm. "Thank you," she said sweetly. She looped her arms in mine and Pippa's. "Well, I guess we better go."

"Where are we going?" I asked as she took us in the opposite direction of the elevators.

"Yeah, I thought the plan was to send Nora in for food, then head up to the room."

"While you were talking to the security guys," Gilly said, "I was watching waitstaff go in and out of a side door near the back."

"And?"

"And, that's our ticket in," Gilly exclaimed. We'll come in at the side with the servers, and then we'll just blend in. We'll eat, we'll drink, and then we'll get the hell out before anyone's the wiser."

"If they catch us," Pippa said, "they are going to throw us out."

"No risk, no reward." Gilly glanced at me. "It's your weekend. Are you up for the challenge?"

I thought about it for half a second. "Lord, we haven't snuck into a place since Milton Farley left the exit door of the Cinema Four cracked open for us. We watched *Ferris Bueller's Day Off.*"

"Whatever happened to Milton?"

"He's an accountant for the IRS," I replied.

Gilly laughed. "Doesn't that fit."

"Are we sneaking into this place or not?" Pippa asked.

I nodded, my sense of adventure strong. "Let's do it."

"There is a service hall down at the end of the corridor, according to the hotel map." Gilly held out a trifold hotel brochure.

A man in a brown uniform, carrying a box, walked past us at a brisk pace. "Excuse me," he said when the corner of the box caught my arm, but he didn't stop.

"Cripes," Pippa said. "That was rude."

"He excused himself," I told her. "Besides, we don't want to draw attention to ourselves by making a fuss."

"There's the service door." Gilly pointed at a security door a few feet from us. Her voice lowered into a conspiratorial whisper. "Let's go."

The door said, "Employees Only," but we ignored its directive and went on in. The hall was not as nice as the guest area. It had an industrial feel with the gray walls and exposed metal. Plus, it smelled dank and musty.

I caught memories of workers hauling equipment, carrying food, pushing carts as we walked along. A young man in a valet uniform raised his eyes at us, and I expected him to call security, but he said, "Are you lost?"

"We're supposed to be going to the Oak Room," Pippa said, with the air of someone who was supposed to be there. "We were told to bring some items in through the service door." Thank heavens, she was cool under pressure.

"Cool." He gestured with a nod over his shoulder. "It's just up the hall."

"Thank you," she said with a pleasant smile.

He shrugged and walked on.

"How do we know which doors belong to what room?" Pippa asked.

I shrugged. "I guess we just check. What's the worst that can happen?"

Pippa shook her head. "We get caught and get thrown out of the conference for trespassing."

"We can go back if you want," I said. "No harm no foul."

She blew out a breath. "In for a penny, in for a pound. I just hope they don't arrest us for trespassing."

"We'll be fine," I reassured her, praying I was right.

"That one is the third, and it's cracked open already," Gilly said, as she scooted ahead of us. "I'll see if the coast is clear." She opened the door and looked inside. "Okay, this is not the Belliza party. I'm pretty sure this is the American version of the Tardis.

"Nope," Pippa agreed when she looked over Gilly's shoulder. "This isn't the party. This is the room where Selebrate is launching the Stress-less," she said in a hushed voice.

"How do you know?" I asked, trying to get a peek around my two taller friends.

Pippa opened the door wider and gestured at the huge sign hanging from the ceiling that said, "Selebrate More and Stress-Less."

"Clever tag line," I said with some respect. "This has to be the Rosewood Room. That's where Gregory said his launch was happening."

"Oh, hey. We passed that room on the way to this hall," Pippa said. "It's the room right next to Oak."

"Then, Oak is probably the next door." I was curious to check out the meditation pod that had been the cause of so much drama. "However, maybe we can take a quick peek at the display."

Pippa stopped short of going through the door. Her cheeks reddened, a flush of anxiety. "We can't go in there. What if someone sees us? Don't they have cameras or something?"

I looked up and down the narrow corridor. "I don't see

any cameras in this service hallway, and even if they do have some, we'll just tell them we took a wrong turn if we get caught. We're three women without any records, and Gilly here is really good at acting ditzy."

"Oh, it's an act, huh?" Pippa teased, her color returning back to normal.

Gilly stuck her tongue out at her.

"Still, maybe we shouldn't—"

"Look, we aren't supposed to go into the Belliza brunch, either, but we're doing it. And, frankly, I want to check out this doomed machine," I said. "But I understand why you guys wouldn't want to go in." I offered a reassuring smile. "No worries. No pressure. Honestly. You all can wait out here for me in the hall, or just go on up to the next door for the party. I'll only be a second."

"Oh, hell no," was Gilly's response. "If you're going in, I'm going in." She brushed past me. "Wow, talk about stepping into the future. This is really cool."

I followed her but suddenly felt hesitant as a sense of foreboding mixed with wonder washed through me.

Maybe the adventurer within me wasn't as strong as I'd thought. I crossed into the event room.

Neon lighting traced the upper and lower curves of the meditation pod, and they lit up the white walls with lines of blue and pink around the perimeter. The word Stress-less glowed green in an oval logo on the side. Monitors lined one wall. There was a round chair that looked as if someone had plucked it out of Jane Jetson's kitchen. Even with the sparse lighting, I could see that every part of the display was white, giving the room a real science fiction vibe. Gilly was right. This was a retro version of a spaceship.

Pippa stood by the table with an aromatherapy diffuser. "What is that smell?" she asked.

I strolled over and sniffed. "It's lemon verbena."

"I know what lemon verbena is," she said. "I meant that sorta burnt...um, Nora?"

*It's dark except for the pod, the monitor, and the colorful aromatherapy diffuser. The water vapors glimmer above the unit and its rotating lights. A movement catches my eye, but I can't see much more than the shadows. Suddenly, someone is standing near the radiant pod.*

*I can't tell for sure, but even with the face area blurry, it looks as if he or she is wearing a ski mask.*

*Gloved hands lift the lid. I see a bright burst of light.*

*Then another.*

*The pod's lights go out...*

Gilly yelped as I came out of the vision. "Cripes almighty," she sobbed. "There's a dead girl in the pod!"

Pippa found a light switch on the wall and flipped it. The bright fluorescence blinded me for a moment. And when I looked at the pod, I saw an unnaturally contracted hand sticking out the side with pearly pink nails and a matching smartwatch that I recognized.

"Oh, my God," I said, my heart beating in my throat. "I think that's Gregory's assistant, Samantha."

# CHAPTER 7

"*H*ow did this happen?" Gilly asked as she backed away from the pod. The pod was shaped like an egg, but it was designed so only your upper body was under the hood. Which meant we could see legs, hips, hands, and forearms, but not her face.

"I don't know. It's awful, though," I said. I surmised it was Samantha from the petal-pink pencil skirt she wore and her pretty pink manicure and matching watch. And if it wasn't her, then it was a hell of a coincidence. Her legs were twisted oddly, and there was a dark scuff on the heel of her shoe.

Gilly pulled a face. "Should we check for a pulse or something?"

Pippa bent down and tapped Samantha's shin. She paled. "She's stiff as a board. How quickly does rigor mortis set in?"

"About two to six hours after death." I shivered. "Are we sure she's dead?"

Pippa went to grab the pod cover to lift it up.

57

"Stop. Don't touch it." Samantha's hand dangled out the side. There was a faint bluish tint to her skin. I walked over and, careful not to touch her smartwatch band or any part of the pod where I might leave fingerprints, I touched the inside of her wrist, right below the base joint of her thumb. I'd taken care of my sick mother long enough to know how to find the radial pulse. Samantha's cold wrist didn't have one. I met Pippa's mortified gaze. "Gilly was right the first time. She's dead."

Pippa blinked, her eyes huge. "Do you think the pod killed her?"

I grimaced. "The pod's lights are on." They'd gone out in my vision when the person in the mask had tinkered with it. "But since I don't really know how it works, it's hard to guess one way or the other." Samantha had inferred that the meditation pod might be a death trap. Had she decided to test drive the pod, and it killed her? "We need to get hotel security. That guy Robson."

"Not the police?" Pippa asked.

"Probably better to let the hotel handle the reporting," I said. "They'll call the police and take it from there."

Pippa's hands were shaking. "Cripes, Nora. I feel like bolting right now."

Wanting to run away was a completely normal response to finding a dead body. "I know. I'm sorry I said we should come in here." I noticed a soft fluffy red thread on the front of Samantha's skirt, but only because it stood out in contrast to the pale pink. Probably just contact lint. I got it on me all the time. "Who wants to go get Robson?"

"I will," Gilly said. She rubbed her arms as if warding off a chill. "I'll be right back."

"I seriously don't want to be here." Pippa didn't look at me. She was staring at the exit door to the Rosewood Room.

"We can step out into the hallway if you want," I said. "But we should go out the way we came in. Are you okay?"

"I've...she's dead. Gosh, Nora. She's so...she was so young. I mean, how in the world could something this awful happen?"

I thought about Fiona McKay. She'd been as young as or younger than Samantha. Only twenty-four years old. A woman with a troubled past, but with her whole future ahead of her. I'd found her body in the Garden Cove lake. Murdered, it turned out, by a sadistic dirty cop and the jealous, bitter woman who'd hired him. Finding her dead in the lake had shaken me. So, I knew precisely how Pippa felt.

"I wish I knew." I gave Pippa's arm a comforting pat.

Pippa wrung her hands. "I'm...numb. I feel like there's something I should be doing right now, but I don't know what." She hugged her arms. "I'm a fixer, Nora. I fix things. You know that. You throw a problem at me, and I'll find solutions. But how do I fix this?"

"You can't, Pip. I'm sorry, but there's nothing for you to fix here."

"Luke is on his way in." Gilly rushed toward us, a little out of breath. When she got to us, she put her hand on my shoulder to steady herself as she picked up her foot and gave it a quick flex and rotations. "My feet are killing me. Why did I wear heels? My plantar fasciitis is really acting up. " She put her foot down and grimaced. "Sorry. That was insensitive. We need to leave the room. Luke wants us to stay put in the hallway."

Pippa glanced at Gilly as we returned to the service hall. "Did he say how long it would take for him to get here?"

"He had to make a call, but said he'd be right behind me." Gilly looked up when the door opened to the hall, and Luke Robson jogged in our direction.

"There he is," she said.

Robson's gaze was sharp and observant as he looked us over. "Who found the body?"

Gilly nodded as she gestured at the three of us. "We all did. It's in this room." She pointed to the closed door.

"She's in the meditation pod," I added. "Her name is Samantha."

"So, you all know the deceased?" Robson asked.

"No," I answered. "I met her for the first time today. But I recognized her nail polish and smartwatch. She works for Gregory Paramount."

Robson arched a brow at me. "Who's that?"

"This is his company's exhibition room," I said. "He's launching the Stress-less pod this weekend."

"So, you know this Samantha's boss?"

I nodded. "But before today, I hadn't seen Gregory in years."

Robson pulled on some purple nitrile gloves. I recognized them because it was the same brand that I used when I worked with dyes in my shop. "I'm going to go check out the situation," he said. "Did any of you touch anything in the room?"

"I felt for a pulse, but I didn't touch any of the equipment in the room."

"I touched the door handle," Gilly offered. She held up her hands. "But nothing else."

Pippa shook her head but didn't speak.

"Pippa tapped her leg," I said. "To see if she was sleeping."

Worry creased Robson's brow. "Wait here, please."

He opened the door and went into the room. We crowded into the opened doorway and watched as he walked to the display and carefully lifted the pod cover and checked for a carotid pulse.

I gasped when he moved out of the way, and we saw her face. It was grayish-blue, and her mouth was gruesomely open as if she'd been screaming. He closed the lid. Next, he examined the scene without disturbing anything in the room.

Next, he went to the wall, turned off the light switch, and pulled a small black light from his pocket. He waved it over the floor around the pod. There were some splotchy-glowy places on the floor. I hadn't seen any blood in the room or on Samantha.

Robson muttered a few words to himself, then shook his head. He turned on the lights again, put away his black light, took off his gloves, then joined us just outside the door. He took a small spiral notepad out of his pocket along with a pencil.

"It's two-ten now. When was the last time you saw this Samantha? Alive, I mean?" he asked.

"Maybe around twelve-thirty," I replied. "She was up on the fourteenth floor having a heated conversation with her boss, Gregory Paramount."

He jotted down my response. "Gregory Paramount," he repeated. "You say they were having an argument?"

I shook my head. "No. An argument takes two people, and this was him being angry about bad news. She told him she'd thought someone had messed with this pod, and he was upset."

He nodded and continued to write.

In the hall, Gregory had threatened to fire her if she didn't get the pod fixed for the launch. Had she done something desperate to make it work? Had she tried to fix the machine herself to see if it and the launch could be salvaged in some way? If Remy Tarlington or Brian Langford sabotaged the machine, did that make one or both of them responsible for Samantha's death even if it was an accident?

"I...I overheard her say the pod might be dangerous if it wasn't fixed. Do you think this could have been accidental?" I asked Robson.

Robson shook his head, his dark hair spilling over his eyes. He pushed it back. At first, I'd thought he was younger, closer to Ezra's age, but I could see now that he had a few age lines around his eyes that gave him the more grizzled look of someone in his forties or fifties. Mostly, Robson looked tired.

"I don't want to speculate. It's the job for the police and the medical examiner," he said. "So, why did you guys go into the room?"

Gilly toed the carpet, then said, "We were on our way to the—" She shrugged. "Honestly, we were going to—"

"We went into the wrong door," I finished. No way I was going to let Gilly or Pippa take on any of this. I'd been the one who wanted to check out the Stress-less. Of course, I thought I'd be in and out. Finding a dead woman hadn't been on the agenda. "My fault. I thought we were heading back toward the elevators."

"You mistook a service hall with a big sign that said 'employees only' for the hall to the elevators?" he asked with a fair amount of skepticism.

"Yep," I said. "I didn't see the sign. I left my reading glasses in the room."

Pippa and Gilly were looking at me with such relief, it made me ache.

Pippa nodded emphatically. "We are always telling Nora she shouldn't go out without her glasses."

"And what about you two? Did you leave your reading glasses in the room?"

"I wasn't paying attention," Gilly said.

"Same," Pippa agreed. "When Nora went through, we just followed."

"Robson, where are you?" a male voice sounded from the radio on his hip.

He unclipped it, held it up to his face and pushed the button on the side. "At the Rosewood Room on the sixth floor, at the service entrance." He let go of the button, his expression plainly adding a "duh" to the end of his response.

Gilly gave him a sympathetic look. He rewarded her with a soft smile.

"My boss," he mouthed.

"Please tell me it's a prank," the boss said.

"No, sir," said Robson. "I'll take the next steps."

"Don't do anything else until I get there," the boss ordered.

"Yes, sir." His phone was in a leather case, also attached to his belt. He retrieved it and began to dial 9-1-1.

"I thought your boss said not to do anything," Gilly said.

"I was an officer in the CID, criminal investigation division, for the United States Army for twenty years before I retired. I'm not waiting for my boss to come down here to double-check my work." After a few seconds, he said into his phone, "This is Luke Robson, Senior Security Specialist for the Frazier Ambassador Hotel. I'd like to report a death on the premises."

* * *

"How DID you get into the room?" Officer Dale Mather asked me. We were out in the main hallway now, with more body and breathing room than the service hall. It was the third time the question had been posed to me.

I wanted to roll my eyes, but I didn't. My father had been the chief of police in Garden Cove, and my boyfriend was a homicide detective. I knew it was standard practice to ask the same questions over and over to make sure they got the same answers. People who tended to change their stories or answers usually became suspects.

"The door was unlocked," I said again. "Gilly opened it, and we all went inside."

I glanced at Gilly and Pippa, who were being interviewed by other police officers. They'd separated us to go over our recall of the events prior to finding Samantha's body.

"We were trying to go to the...uhm, elevators. But it was my mistake. Wrong door, wrong hall, wrong everything situation." I was trying to be extremely cooperative without getting us into trouble, so we could extricate ourselves from the situation as soon as possible. I hoped Gilly and Pippa were doing the same. The last thing I wanted was to be involved in another death investigation. "We basically entered the room together."

"Because you thought it led to the elevators?" he asked, his tone suspicious.

I offered him a shrug and a smile but didn't answer the question. The less I said, the better.

"Okay," Mathers said. "Wait here."

Having us here wasn't going to help the police at this point. Our knowledge was limited to the few minutes we'd entered the room, found Samantha, checked for a pulse, and called for help. Right now, we were more of a distraction than anything else. "Can we go back to our room?"

"We're about done. You can go back to your room, but make sure you're available if we have more questions."

He was serious, as he should be. Still, I resisted the urge to salute him. "No problem, Officer Mathers."

"What's going on here?" I heard Gregory ask.

I glanced up to see Robson blocking him from getting

closer. With him was an older gentleman with a silver-haired combover and Carmen. She clutched her purse to her chest, her face pale as she met my gaze. Aaron, her assistant, was off to the side, staring out a window over-looking downtown and talking on his phone. He glanced over a few times, his eyes darting back to the view.

I cast a sympathetic look at Gregory. I'm not sure how close he and Samantha were, but Pippa had been my assistant, and I loved her like family. Sure, he'd been snippy with Samantha, but sometimes that happened in times of high stress. If Samantha and Gregory had developed even a small portion of the bond I had with Pip, this would be a devastating loss.

Robson, after being ordered to do so by the silver-haired man, explained the facts of the situation.

"That door was supposed to be locked," Gregory said. "How in the world did anyone get inside?" Gregory looked at me when he asked the question.

He'd been friendly the first time we'd spoken today, contrite the next, but now he looked pissed.

Robson shook his head. "According to the witnesses, the door was unlocked."

"The service door," the silver-haired man amended.

"Yes," Robson said. "The service door."

"Poor Samantha," Carmen said. "Will you cancel the launch party now?"

Gregory gave her a sharp look. "What's happened is terrible, but I can't cancel this launch. There is too much at stake for Selebrate." He rounded his shoulders in a posturing move I'd seen him take during tough negotia-tions. He might have been directing his speech to

Robson, but he was talking to me. "And what were the witnesses doing in the room in the first place?"

When Robson didn't answer immediately, the silver-haired man blustered. "Well, Robson," he asked him. "What do you have to say?"

Robson shrugged and repeated my lie. "According to Ms. Black, they entered by accident."

Gregory narrowed his gaze on me. He let out a slow breath, the lines around his eyes relaxing before he said, "Ms. Black never struck me as the kind of woman who does things by accident."

# CHAPTER 8

"So, do we want to keep our dinner reservation at Darbie's?" I asked. We'd already rescheduled our massages for Saturday morning. I felt bad. Gilly and Pippa had made a real effort to put this weekend together as a birthday getaway for me, but finding Samantha dead had put a damper on the weekend. If my two BFFs felt anything like I did, then going to Darbie's now felt wrong. "Or do you all just want to stay in and order room service?"

"It's your weekend, Nora. Whatever you want to do," Pippa said. She began to gather clothes from the drawer. "I'll shower first."

" I vote for room service tonight. We'll get a bottle of wine. We'll chat. It'll be nice."

Gilly let out a breath and forced a smile. "Yes. Let's do it."

Pippa nodded then shook her head. "Great. It'll be a relief not to have to get dressed up tonight. I can't wait to get out of these clothes and into some comfy pajamas."

"For me, it's the bra." Gilly reached into the collar of her loose-fitting top and grabbed the straps of her bra and gave them a tug. "The curse of big boobs. But first, I'll go and get some ice for the sodas."

"I put a few of your Diet Cokes in the refrigerator earlier," I said. "They should be cold."

"When we order room service, no wine for me tonight," Pippa said. "Just order some lemon-lime soda for me." She pushed on her belly. "My stomach is a little bloop-bloop."

"You're not coming down with something, are you?"

"Nothing like that," she assured me.

My watch vibrated. I looked down and rolled my eyes at the bastard. It was reminding me to get up and move. "I've walked enough today, jerk."

"Who are you talking to?" Pippa asked.

"This smartwatch. It nags me if I don't get in two-hundred and fifty steps every hour during the day. It wants me to get up and get going."

"My get-up-and-go got up and went," Gilly quipped.

Pippa and I stared at her. A burble of laughter erupted from Pippa. I tried not to laugh as well, but it spread through the room like a virus, catching Gilly and me. The term hysterical laughter was not far off the mark.

Once we could all breathe, after several failed attempts to stop, Pippa started crying. Gilly and I hugged her.

"I'm sorry." Pippa dabbed at her eyes. "What is wrong with me?"

"I get it." I patted her back. "There's no right or wrong way to react here."

"Are we going to be able to salvage this weekend?" Gilly asked.

"What happened to Samantha was most likely an accident." I wasn't sure I believed that one hundred percent, but it would be up to the police to determine, not me. "And while it's tragic," I continued, "it doesn't have anything to do with us. Not really." I pulled back my shoulders. "But if you don't think you can be here, Pippa, you tell us, and we will pack our stuff and go tonight."

Pippa nodded on a sniff. "I'm okay to stay. Besides, didn't Officer Mathers tell us to stick around?"

"He's got our phone numbers, and it's only a two-hour ride back if he needed us in person. But I'm good with staying." I gave her another brief hug then sat on the edge of the bed. "We'll eat, drink, and talk until we fall asleep." I stretched my neck and rubbed the knot developing on the left side.

Gilly sat down next to me. "I can give you a neck massage if you want."

"I'm not putting you to work," I told her. "It's not your fault."

"I talked you into sneaking into a party you already had a pass for," she said. "We could have been blissfully unaware right now if we had stuck to the plan where you grab all the good food, and we reap the benefits in the room."

"Along with mini-bar wine," Pippa added. "Speaking of." She took a bottle out and unscrewed the top.

"So classy," I said with a smile.

"That's me. I'm a classy bitch." Pippa waggled the

open bottle at me, then frowned. She screwed the cap back on. "Actually, I don't want any."

I'd noticed since she'd started dating Jordy she hadn't been drinking as much. Maybe because he was a recovering addict and alcoholic. He'd been sober for a long while now, but addiction could rear its ugly head when you least expected it. Still, if she wanted to stay dry, I'd make it easy on her. "Stomach upset still?"

She paled and nodded.

Gilly pressed her shoulder against mine. "Maybe we can go down to the sauna after we eat."

The idea of a nice heated sauna to loosen my muscles sounded good. "It's better than a sharp stick in the eye."

"I'll probably just lie down for a bit after we eat," Pippa said.

I noticed she hadn't said much about Jordy. "Is everything okay with you and Jordy?"

Pippa's eyes widened. "Yes, of course. It's...things are really good." Her pensive expression worried me.

"Okay," I said, letting it go. For now.

"That security guy was nice, didn't you think?" Gilly asked out of the blue.

"He was," I agreed. I gave her a half-smile. "Is there some chemistry there?"

"Stop." She covered her mouth on a giggle. "I was kidding this afternoon when I was asking about Gregory. I meant it when I said I was off men."

"I know," I told her. I patted her leg. "Luke Robson is cute, though."

"And he has a really nice ass," Gilly added.

"I wasn't looking, but I'll take your word for it." I got

up and checked my phone. "Speaking of nice butts, I have three text messages from Ezra."

"Did he really send you a picture of his full moon?" She tried to grab the phone away from me, so I stood up and blocked her with my backside while we played a good old-fashioned game of keep away.

"He didn't send me any naked pictures," I protested.

Pippa sauntered past us as if she were going to the bathroom. "You two are ridiculous." When she was just to the left of me, Gilly distracted me with a grab to the right, and when I moved my arm back and away from her, Pippa nabbed the phone out of my outstretched hand. "Gotcha!" she said.

"No!" I squealed. Keep-away had turned into a game of monkey in the middle. With me jumping...well, more like bouncing up on my toes, waving my arms like a lunatic between my two taller friends as they kept the phone just out of reach.

Pippa held the phone over my head, and she and Gilly laughed and laughed.

I got some air on a bounce and came down with a jolt to the knee. "Ow, ow."

Pippa's arm came down. "Are you okay?"

"Watch her," Gilly said.

But too late, I snatched my phone back. "Hah!"

I limped over to the bed and sat down. I noticed the GPS on my smartwatch tracker app had kicked on. It was automatic anytime my heart rate went up for more than a minute. I smiled as I remembered it tracking Ezra and me out to the boat dock behind his house the night before last. We hadn't gone any farther than the dock. Even so,

I'd had a notification on my phone when we'd returned to his cabin congratulating me for fifty-seven minutes of cardio. Ezra had deserved all the accolades, and later, he'd followed up with an encore that would have made Jane Fonda breathless.

"Seriously," Pippa said. "How's your knee?"

The pain wasn't horrible. "Just a little tweak is all. A couple ibuprofen and I'll be right as rain." I put on my glasses and unlocked my phone screen. What I saw made me smile.

"What does Detective Hot Stuff have to say?" Gilly asked, crowding me so she could see. "Let me live vicariously."

"He says he loves me, and he misses me."

"Uhm." Gilly smirked. "From what I see, he misses your smell, your taste, your—"

"That's enough," I gently chided. I couldn't keep the grin off my face. "Ezra misses all that."

Pippa picked up her phone, unlocked the screen, and smiled.

"Jordy?" I asked.

She held out the screen for us to see. It was a picture of Jordy, shirtless, with all his tattoos on display, on his bed with his two dogs, a black American Staffordshire named Bo and a sweet basset hound named Helma. The caption read, *wanna cuddle?*

"That's so sweet," I said, feeling all loved up for my girl, and less concerned about my earlier fear that she and Jordy were having problems. "He adores you."

"I love him, Nora. I love him so much my teeth hurt."

"I know a good dentist," Gilly said with a laugh. "You both look happy."

I met her gaze. "I am super happy." Dead girl aside, I hadn't been this happy in a long time. Even so, I wondered what would have happened if Mom hadn't gotten cancer. "You know, sometimes I think about my old life. Where I would be if I hadn't moved back to Garden Cove."

"And?" Pippa asked, sitting down on the other side of me.

"And I don't know." I glanced back down at Ezra's text. "I love where I'm at, and I love who I'm with, and my friends..." I put my head on Gilly's shoulder and my arm around Pippa. "I can't imagine not seeing you guys all the time."

We paused for a moment of reflection, then Gilly said, "Did you get any of your aroma mojo when we were in the room? You zoned out for a few seconds."

"Did you?" Pippa asked. "Did you see anything that pointed to foul play?"

Cripes. I'd almost forgotten about the vision. Sometimes, the way they played in my head was virtually like fleeting thoughts. "I did see something," I affirmed. "Nothing about what happened to Samantha, but I did see something. The lemon verbena scent triggered a vision of someone in a ski mask tampering with the pod. He or she lifted the lid, and there was a spark. At least, I suspect they were tampering, otherwise, why wear a mask?"

"You know, we could look into this," Pippa said. "I

could speak to Aaron. Nora, you could get a little closer to Gregory and Carmen."

I made an "ew" face.

"Gilly can use her charm on the sexy security guy."

"You mean ex-Army officer Luscious Luke Robson?" I asked.

Gilly smiled. "Sexy security guy works." She nodded. "I'm in."

I looked at my gold badge on the media desk in our room. "I'm calling Blanche to get you guys your badges. If we're going to do a little digging, we'll need wider access."

"Damn, Nora. You talk like you were raised by a cop," Gilly said.

"And married to one," Pippa added.

"And am currently dating one," I finished. "You guys are hilarious." I clapped my hands together. "Okay. I'll call Blanche. Gilly, order dinner. I'll take anything on the menu with bacon. And Pippa..."

She looked at me. "Yes?"

I struggled to think of a third immediate thing. "Stay beautiful."

Pippa flashed a smile at me. "Aww. Thanks, babe. How about if I jump in the shower while you two are doing all that."

"It's a plan." My watch buzzed me again. I sighed. "I'm going to call Blanche while I take a lap around the hall."

"And maybe call Ezra after, for some sexy talk," Gilly said.

I stood up with my phone in hand. "You do exercise your way, and I'll do it mine."

# CHAPTER 9

*G*illy hadn't been wrong about me calling Ezra. I actually called him as soon as I left the room, holding off on contacting Blanche for a few minutes.

My guy picked up on the first ring. "Hey, darling. Having fun?" I could hear the smile in his voice, and it sent a thrill through my body.

"Sure," I said with fake chipper. "So much fun."

"What's wrong?"

I wanted to tell him, but I also didn't want him to worry about me. "Why would you think anything's wrong?"

"You get this pinched sound in your voice when you're stressed."

"I do, huh?"

He chuckled softly. "What's wrong, sweetheart?"

Would he tell me to come home? Would he warn me off getting involved? I hoped not. I'd had enough men in my past who tried to control me "for my own good." I didn't want that kind of relationship. "We found some-one...someone who died," I told him.

There was a long pause. Finally, Ezra said, "Are you being serious?"

"As a heart attack." I was nervous about his reaction. "Or in this case, probably an accidental death."

"Did you know the deceased?"

"Not really. I met her when I got here today. She's the assistant..." I shook my head. "She was the assistant for a man..." How far did I take the honesty route? I sighed. All the freaking way. "A man I used to date."

There was only a micropause before Ezra said, "You want to tell me about it?"

"About Gregory?"

"Is he the deceased woman?" he teased.

I coughed. "No. He's my ex."

"You can tell me about him, too, if you want. Anything you want to talk to me about, I'm here for it, Nora." His voice calmed my inner wild and eased the stress knot in my neck eased a little. I guess I was still learning to trust Ezra. Or maybe myself. Ezra had never been the "let me fix it for you, little lady" type.

"I want to tell you about him, about her, about every-thing. It's been a strange day." I explained about the Remy altercation, the vision, ice machine alcove convo, the pod sabotage, Blanche, the VIP pass, and the fatefully opened door, and our plan to do a little investigating to see what we could find out. "After all," I said, "I feel like we owe Samantha. Because finding her..."

"Makes her your responsibility," he finished.

"In a way. Yes," I said.

"Anything else?" he asked.

"Nope, not unless you count two people having sex in the ice machine alcove."

"When did this happen?" He snorted a laugh. "And why were you there?"

"I wasn't there. It was a vision."

He laughed again. "I figured."

"So, what do you think?" I held my breath, hoping Ezra wouldn't disappoint me.

He didn't. "I think this Samantha and her family are lucky that you were the one who found her."

"Really?"

"Really. You're a smart woman with a keen mind and, well, let's face it, a gift made for investigation. If anyone can get to the truth of what happened to this girl, it's you."

Ezra, once again, didn't disappoint me in the least. "You mean it, don't you?"

"Nora Black, I say what I mean and mean what I say."

"I like that about you."

His voice went sly. "What else do you like about me?"

"I like the way your tone dips when you say my name."

"Anything else?"

"I like the way your green eyes sparkle when you look at me."

"Go on," he said.

"I like how good you are with your hands."

"You mean my ability to unsnap bras and buttons with two fingers."

"Among other things." I rounded the final corner, walking back toward the suite. "I like your lips."

"Tell me about them."

"The way they feel on my— Oh." I halted abruptly as I was suddenly face-to-face with Gregory. "Can I call you back later?"

He chuckled. "Sure thing. I'd love to finish this conversation."

I was glad the sexy talk with Ezra hadn't gotten too explicit or smacking into my ex-boyfriend could have been super embarrassing. "Terrific. It's a date."

"I love you, Nora," he said with such sweet sincerity, my heart melted.

"I love you," I replied, then disconnected.

Gregory watched me as I finished my call, then said, "Can I talk to you?"

"Oh, okay. Sure." I gave him a sympathetic smile as I put my phone in my pocket. After all, his assistant had just died. Still, it was strange that I kept running into him. "I was just stretching my legs. My room is just over there."

He shoved his hands in his pockets. "I know. I knocked. Your friends told me you were walking around. I've been waiting for you."

"What can I do for you?"

Gregory peered down at me, his expression tense. "Did you take...um, anything from the Rosewood Room?"

The question took me by surprise. Was he worried I stole a few aromatherapy samples? "No," I said firmly.

He moved closer to me, and it felt aggressive. I stepped around him so that he was no longer between me and my room door. "What about your friends?"

I took my keycard from my pocket and fidgeted with the corner. "They didn't take anything, either."

Gregory reached out and grabbed my wrist. Dark half-circles of worry had formed under his red-rimmed eyes. I saw the grief there, and the anger. "Are you spying on me, Nora?"

I yanked my wrist out of his grip and backed away. I caught a whiff of eucalyptus and cedarwood from Gregory's jacket sleeve, then...

*"Christ, what is this stuff?" a man asks. He is wearing a ball cap, so I can't see his hair color, and his voice is low. Too soft and quiet to recognize. "It's pungent."*

*"It's Rel-action," a dark-haired woman replies. They are in a suite, much like the one I share with my BFFs. So I know the memory unfolding takes place in the Frazier Hotel. She puts a pink tablet on the desk. I recognize her hair, her fingernails, and her watch. Samantha.*

*"Rel-action?" The man snorts. "What kind of name is that?"*

*"It an aromatherapy scent for the new pod. One of the bottles broke in my suitcase. I have to take the rest down to the display room tonight so the tech can set it up. It's a combination of relaxation and action."*

*The man grabs her around the waist and pulls her close. She's giggling as he nuzzles her neck. "I don't feel relaxed," he says, his voice low and growly. "But I'm definitely ready for action."*

*"Are we really doing this?" she asks him. "It's dangerous."*

*"No risk, no reward." He nuzzles her neck. "Do you trust me?"*

*She leans her head back and moans as he works his way lower. "I do," she tells him. "I really do."*

Gregory stared at me, frowning. "What's wrong? You look out of it."

"Nothing's wrong with me." My brain was spinning. It took me a second to compose my thoughts. Gregory hadn't been the man in Samantha's vision, so how could the scent memory be tied to him? Had he been in the room? No. Every time I had a memory, I always saw the person attached to the scent. So how?

I rubbed my skin where Gregory had grabbed me. He'd never acted aggressive or violent in any way when we'd dated. Not even when I broke up with him. Of course, that didn't mean anything right now. "But there's something definitely wrong with you."

"I..." He glanced at my wrist, shame flooding his expression. "I'm sorry. Look, the police questioned me about my conversation with Samantha on this very floor today. There was no one around when we were talking, yet, you know all about it. Why is that, Nora? Are you a spy? Was leaving Belliza a ruse? Are you working for Konash? Are you working for the enemy?"

The questions flew at me like attacking birds, and I saw the other Gregory—the grabby, manhandling one—in the fury etched on his face. I didn't like that I was scared, but I wasn't a fool, either.

I turned and dashed to my hotel room door and pounded on it. I had the keycard in my other hand, but I was quaking so hard, I didn't think I could use it.

Gilly opened the door. Pippa, hair in a towel, stood right behind her. I bustled my way inside.

"Nora! Wait!"

I turned as Gregory stopped short and then moved back. He looked like he wanted to grab me again and shake me until the answers fell out of my mouth.

"Did either of you take anything from the Rosewood Room?" I asked, my glare burning a hole in Gregory.

"No," they both said.

Pippa's eyes narrowed. "Why would we?"

"Because we're corporate spies, apparently." Now that I had my friends at my back, I felt less threatened. I pointed my finger at my accuser. "We don't work for Konash or anyone else. I was in the ice machine alcove when you were talking to Samantha earlier today. I am not a part of whatever conspiracy, reality or fantasy-based, that you've concocted in your paranoid brain."

Gregory scrubbed his face with his hands, then made a sound of frustration. When he looked at us again, I saw genuine remorse reflected in his gaze. "I'm really sorry." He turned on his heel and slunk off down the hall.

"That guy is losing it," Gilly said as she and Pippa pulled me farther into the room and shut the door.

I let out a deep sigh then pulled my shoulders back. The memory I'd had was of Samantha and a man she was having a fling with, but who? I would have recognized Gregory right away by his voice and build. Even so, the man had seemed familiar. If Samantha's lover wasn't Gregory, then how the heck had I seen Samantha's memory when I smelled the odor on him?

The scent on his cuff belonged to Samantha. Not him. So, had he been in Samantha's room? Dug around in her things? And if so, was that before or after her death?

"Why does he think we stole whatever-it-was?" Pippa asked.

"Because we were in the room with his dead assistant." My throat suddenly dry, I went to the sink and poured myself a cup of water. I took a sip. "Honestly, I don't remember seeing anything in that room important enough for him to accost me in the hallway. Did Samantha have it? Maybe he thought we'd rifled through her pockets."

"Well, locked room or not, the thingie-ma-doo shouldn't have been in there. Especially after they suspected the pod had been sabotaged."

"That's a desperate dude," Gilly said.

"His intensity was frightening." My head swooned. I leaned against the sink counter just inside the room. "I've never seen him act that way before."

"Girl, you just turned fifty shades of pale. Sit," Gilly ordered. She took me by the elbow, and I let her lead me to the nearest bed. I sat on the edge.

"I'm fine. Just a little woozy. I had a vision when Gregory grabbed me."

"Did you see him kill Samantha?" Pippa asked, eyes wider than dinner plates.

"No," I said. "But that doesn't mean he didn't have something to do with her death."

# CHAPTER 10

*Friday, August 8th...*
The next morning, the spotlight of the rising sun coming through the open window was a visual alarm. Which meant we were already up by the time our wakeup call came at six-thirty. Our suite window faced the east, and no one had thought to close the curtains when we finally—after a round of hotel burgers and steak fries, several mini bottles of wine, and some girl talk—settled down to sleep.

"We need to remember to close the curtain tonight," I grumbled as I shielded my eyes from the glaring morning sun. I saw my phone was at fifteen-percent battery. Crap. I'd forgotten to put it on the charger. A sheepish smile turned up my lips as I remembered tipsy-dialing Ezra from the shower sometime after the girls went to sleep.

"Here's a cup of coffee." Gilly handed me a steaming mug. "Why are you smiling?"

I shrugged and took a sip. The coffee was smooth, with no hint of bitterness, and the aroma was slightly

WAR OF THE NOSES

nutty. In other words, divine. "Wow, the hotel has great coffee."

"No, I have great coffee," Gilly corrected. " I brought my own one-cup coffee maker and a variety bag of coffee and tea cartridges for it. That's the Central American select. It's a medium-dark roast with hints of nut and cocoa."

"It's one-hundred percent amazing."

"Now who's glad I packed so much?"

"I am," Pippa said. "I want some hot tea with sugar."

Gilly affected a bad British accent. "How very pip-pip of you." She smiled, then nodded. "Coming right up."

I groaned as I sat all the way up. "How can you be so perky? My head is sloshy after last night."

"I drink more wine than you do, so I have a higher tolerance," Gilly suggested.

I choked on my sip of coffee. "I'm not sure that's something to brag about."

"I have a very particular set of skills," she said, blasé. "Skills I have acquired over my long years of wine drinking. Skills that allow me to drink responsibly and not get a hangover."

"You have to stop watching *Taken*."

"Liam Neeson is my boyfriend," Gilly said.

"You really do have the worst taste in men," Pippa said on a laugh.

Gilly finished pouring the water into the one-cup coffee maker, and hit the start button, walked over to Pippa's bed and threw a pillow at her. "What's wrong with Liam Neeson?"

85

I cleared my throat. "Speaking of agendas," I said, to change the subject. "What's our morning look like?"

Pippa grabbed her phone and pulled up the schedule. She scrolled with her index finger. "Breakfast ends at nine-thirty, so we can take our time getting ready."

"Yay." I was in no hurry to jump up from the bed.

Pippa spread her fingertips across the screen and enlarged the text. "We have the PDO Threads demonstration at ten."

"What the heck is that?" I asked. "And you can borrow my reading glasses if you want."

"I don't need reading glasses," Pippa said.

I remembered being resistant when my vision started to go. I did a lot of compensating for a few years before I finally saw an ophthalmologist. Now it felt like my farsighted vision kept getting worse every day. "Okay. So, what's this PDA thingy?"

"Gilly picked the class," Pippa said, in "not it" fashion.

"It's PDO. Not PDA." Gilly became very animated. "PDA is a public display of affection. PDO threads are used for a nonsurgical facelift where they place these sugar threads in strategic places under your skin in your face that lift and build collagen naturally as they dissolve. It's super cool, and I want to see it in action." She touched her neck and cheeks. "It's supposed to last for a year or so."

I scoffed, but my curiosity was peaked. I'd noticed lately that my jawline was losing its firmness, my eyelids drooped, and my upper lip had gotten thinner. I wasn't opposed to the idea of plastic surgery, a nip here or there, eventually, but not until I was much older. But something like this could be an interesting alternative. Still... "I'll believe it when I see it," I finally said.

"Don't even try to fool me, Nora Black." Gilly grinned. "I know you're interested."

I chuckled. "I really am."

Pippa grabbed her tea. "Now that we have gold badges —thank you, Blanche—our convention options are a lot better."

"Here, here." I raised my coffee cup. Blanche had to work an event last night, but she'd been kind enough to have the badges delivered around the same time that our room service had arrived. "All hail Blanche."

Gilly and Pippa toasted with their coffee and tea.

"Anyways, now that we have these golden tickets, we are going to do this convention Willy Wonka style," I said.

"Which part? The part where we turn into giant blueberries or the part where we get sucked up into chocolate tubes?" Gilly asked.

"Candy is dandy, but liquor is quicker," Pippa said, quoting a line from the movie. "As you all found out last night."

We high-fived.

Gilly rolled her eyes. "Go on," she told Pippa. "What's gold get us?"

Pippa gave Gilly a sly look. "The Londa Angelista VIP Room, for one."

Gilly lit up like Vegas at dusk. "Yay! I want one of her bags of goodies so much. I read online that she had like a couple hundred dollars' worth of makeup and beauty products in her bags last year."

"Splendid," I said. "What else?"

"After that is lunch." Pippa squinted her eyes at her phone, then made the text even bigger.

"Are you sure you don't need my glasses?" I teased.

"No," she denied. "My eyesight is fine. The print is just exceedingly small."

"Uh-huh, sure." Gilly and I giggled.

There were a lot of perks to getting older. Giving less of a damn what people thought, more self-assurance, and while I didn't always know what I wanted from my life, I had a much clearer picture of the things that I didn't want. Unfortunately, with the good came the bad. Like hyperopia, for instance.

Watching her scroll through the schedule on her phone while talking about eyewear made me think of Samantha Jones and her glasses, how she would push them up her nose when she—

"Oh," I said with some excitement.

"What is it?" Pippa asked. "Did you have one of your scratch-in-sniff episodes?"

"Not exactly. This time it's my memory." Which I admit wasn't always great since my surgery, but this recall was clear as day. "Both times I saw Samantha, she was holding a pink tablet with a unicorn sticker on the back. Hugging it like it was a treasured woobie. Even in the vision, she'd kept her tablet close. Did either of you see one of those in the Stress-less room?" I asked my friends. "Hers was pink. Probably ten inches," I guesstimated.

"It was pretty sparse in there," Pippa said. "There was the display, of course, and the desktop computer and monitor."

"The aromatherapy diffuser," Gilly added. "But I didn't see anything like a tablet either. And considering almost everything in the space but the lights were white, a pink tablet would have stuck out like a sore thumb. Do you think it's important?"

I nodded. "I bet Samantha's tablet is the thing Gregory was looking for last night."

"Why didn't he just ask if we'd seen her tablet?" asked Gilly irritably. "Why all the secrecy?"

"I read in the Stress-less brochure that the meditation pod has an electromagnetic field that's supposed to work with the body's electrical energy, but it's not good for tech," Pippa said. "She wouldn't have taken it into the pod with her."

"I can't see her leaving it in her room. She seemed attached to the device." I stood up. "Also, she had her smartwatch on. And it's the expensive version. How come she didn't take it off?"

"Oversight?" Pippa answered. "Maybe she just forgot to take it off."

I shook my head. "Things just don't add up for me. I think there's something more than bad sushi going on here."

"Samantha's death might not have been an accident," Gilly said, her voice suddenly hoarse.

"Exactly." My phone beeped and flashed an angry red light at me. Five percent battery. I put it on the charger.

Pippa smirked. "You know, if you're going to have phone sex in a room with two other people, you might turn the shower on next time to cut down on the noise."

My ears burned with a flush of embarrassment. "Oh my God, I hate you right now. And I wasn't being loud."

"Don't worry." Gilly snorted a laugh. "We gave you very high marks for creativity."

I cast her a scandalized glance. "Et tu, Gill-ay?"

"That's the kind of energy I'd love for you to have on our CraftTube videos," Pippa said. "Very enthusiastic."

I put my hands over my ears. "La la la, I can't hear you."

"I wish we could've said the same," Gilly lamented.

"Why didn't you guys knock or something?"

"By the time we knew what was going on, it would have been rude to interrupt," Pippa replied.

Gilly guffawed. "Besides, I have a rule. If the hotel bathroom is a-rockin', I don't bother knockin'." She and Pippa fist-bumped.

I threw myself down on the bed and put a pillow over my head. "Just kill me now."

"We're kidding." Gilly put her hand on my back and gave me a pat. "You're very easy."

"That's what he said," Pippa gibed. She and Gilly giggled again. "Seriously. We were just guessing. You're not the only one who can pick up on clues."

I uncovered my head. "Okay, Sherlock." I threw the pillow at her. "Speaking of clues. We should split up at some point today and do a little digging. I'll go make nice with Gregory. Gilly, you go flirt with the cute security guy, see if you can find out if he knows how Samantha died, and Pippa, you question Aaron."

"This might have been a bad idea," Pippa said. "Maybe we should leave it to the professionals."

"We're not going to do anything that crosses a line."

"Sometimes the line crosses us," Gilly said. "The last time you got involved in an investigation, you almost got killed."

"And a swirly," Pippa added.

I grimaced. The woman responsible for Fiona McKay's death had drugged me and tried to drown me in a public toilet. "This won't be that. If at any time you guys feel weird about a situation, we'll stop investigating."

"Yeah, sure," Gilly said. "As long as we don't have to tackle anyone trying to kill you, we'll call it a win."

# CHAPTER 11

"Holy crap, this is a lot of people," Gilly said. "I mean, I thought yesterday was crowded, but this is a whole new level."

The vendor floor was packed with bodies. We'd just finished a buffet breakfast courtesy of VIP gold, and we'd filled ourselves to the brim with carbs and coffee.

"I don't think the eggs are sitting well," Pippa said as she rubbed her stomach.

"I told you not to eat eggs off a buffet. This is years of con experience talking," I told her as we weaved through the milling bodies. "Where are we going?"

"Ugh. Why didn't I listen? The PDO Thread demo is just around the corner." Pippa pointed to the end of the hall. "Hey, there's Aaron," she said.

He was behind a pillar talking to someone I couldn't see. "Who's he with?"

Pippa shook her head. "I can't tell." She belched. "Sorry. Damn, those eggs."

"Do you need to go back to the room?"

"No, I'm fine. My mission is Aaron, and I'm on it."

"What about the PDO threads?" Gilly whined.

"We still have a few minutes before it starts," I told her.

"We're already going to get terrible seats," she complained.

"Well, if someone hadn't taken an hour to do her hair and makeup," Pippa reminded her. "We could have gone to breakfast a lot earlier." She pressed her fingers to her chest and frowned. "When the eggs were fresher."

Gilly shook her head. "They were never fresh. You think the hotel cracks a thousand eggs a day for a breakfast buffet? They're powdered." She shooed Pippa. "Go. Talk to Aaron."

"Aaron," Pippa said, voice raised to get over the crowd.

He glanced at Pippa, his face tense. Whoever he was with thrust something into Aaron's hand, took off around the backside of the pillar and disappeared in the crowd.

Aaron's fingers closed into a fist around the object, and he slid it into his leather satchel. His smile was forced when he greeted Pippa. "Hey, what's up?"

"We're heading to the PDO Threads demo," Pippa said with more enthusiasm than I thought possible for her and her yucky tummy. "It's so nice to see you, you know, since..." She made a few awkward gestures with her hands to indicate she was talking about Samantha's death.

His eyes glazed over a little. "Yeah, it's just awful."

"Did you know Samantha well?" Pippa asked.

"Our bosses are engaged so..."

"Trust me, I've done my fair share of coordinating schedules with other assistants," Pippa said with the hint of a smile. "Nothing bonds you like being in the trenches."

I cleared my throat. "It's a job, not a war."

They both laughed at me.

"Says someone who's never been an assistant," Aaron said.

I shrugged. "Well, I was never that bad."

Pippa snorted. "Says who?"

"Well, you followed me to Garden Cove, didn't you?"

"And I would do it a hundred times over." She put her hand on my shoulder and gave me a gentle squeeze.

Pippa had quit her job with Belliza to work with me, but I knew that, lately, it was more than work that kept her around. She was in love. I'd known her for over ten years. While Pippa occasionally dated, this was the first time she'd been in a relationship.

"Okay," Aaron said. "I'm jealous. Do you have room at your shop for one more?"

"I thought you were up for a promotion," I replied.

Aaron's expression darkened. "Maybe."

"So," Pippa said with a pensive sigh. "Have you heard how Samantha died?"

He shook his head. "I overheard Gregory say she must have been shocked by the pod. But how in the world could that have happened?" He paled. "Her face was blue. Is that something that happens with electrocution?" His pocket beeped. He reached in and pulled out his phone. "Shoot. What time is it?"

"It's almost ten o'clock."

He shook his head. "I gotta go. My taxi is here."

Was he leaving the hotel? Wouldn't the police have

wanted him to stick around since he knew Samantha? Or, maybe they'd already determined it was an accident. Even so, I worked to keep the alarm out of my voice. "Where are you going?"

"Have to pick up Carmen's pantsuit from the cleaner on the other side of the flipping city," he grumbled.

Gilly clucked her tongue. "What's she doing bringing dirty clothes on a business trip?"

"It's her jumper from yesterday," Aaron corrected. "She spilled wine on it, and it's silk crepe."

I recalled the red jumper with the deep vee in the front. It had looked stunning on Carmen. "I can see why she wanted to get it cleaned right away." But I didn't understand why she sent it to a dry cleaner across town. "Isn't there a dry cleaner here in the hotel?"

Aaron nodded. "She ripped a hole in one of the pockets with that gigantic rock on her engagement ring, so she needed a tailor as well," he said absently before turning his attention to Pippa. "Can we get lunch tomorrow? Or are you busy?"

"I'm having lunch with Gilly and Nora," she said. "It's Nora's birthday tomorrow."

The young man brightened and beamed a smile at me. "Happy Birthday, Nora."

"Thanks." I glanced at Pippa. "You can join us if you want, Aaron." Pippa cast me an unkind look. I grimaced and gave her a slight shrug before diverting my attention back to Aaron. "We have the whole weekend to celebrate. I'm happy to share my friends for an hour."

"Where and when?"

"Darbie's, here in the hotel," I said. "One o'clock tomorrow."

He gave me a quick salute. "Sounds great." His phone beeped again. "I better go." He shuffled past us and hurried away through the crowd.

"Oh, thank heavens." Gilly took my elbow with one hand and Pippa's elbow with her other and ushered us toward the end of the hall. "I thought he'd never leave. We're late as it is."

"I can't believe you invited him to lunch," Pippa hissed.

"Gilly and I will be there, and it will give us a chance to gather more information so that we can ask pertinent questions." I thought my reasoning was sound. Pippa had other ideas.

"I don't want to spend an entire lunch with him looking at me with those puppy dog eyes."

"You don't have to adopt him," I said.

We finally arrived at the room. "I'd like you all to quit arguing for the next fifty minutes," Gilly said with a sigh. "I swear if it's too late for us to join—" She opened the door a crack and looked inside. "Good. People are still getting settled. Let's go find a place to sit."

We found three chairs up against the side wall near the back of the room. Gilly cursed me as she took the one closest to the staging area. There was a huge white screen front and center, and a podium off to the side where a woman with long blonde hair and a white doctor's coat stood. She looked as if she'd had work done, lips a little too full, cheekbones prominent, and eyes tight, but not so much that she looked unnatural. In other words, she'd had an outstanding plastic surgeon.

"Who is that?" I asked.

"That's Mary Graves," Gilly said. She showed us a picture of the woman inside the convention guide. "According to this, she's an aesthetics nurse who specializes in helping women and men to become better versions of themselves."

Gilly's tone conveyed an awe that made me nervous for her. "You know you're stunning, right?"

"Gorgeous," Pippa agreed. "You have skin that most women would kill for."

"You mean women my age," Gilly said.

Pippa's expression soured. "Don't put words in my mouth. I mean women. Period."

I looked at my oldest best friend, who I had known since kindergarten. Her eyes had a few creases at the corners, slight laugh lines around her mouth. Her nose had spread a little over the years, not unlike my own, but she'd manage to maintain a youthful plump to her skin that I envied. Even so, I wasn't about to make her feel any shame if she wanted work done. "I think you're beautiful, but I know it's not about me or what I think."

Gilly rewarded me with a slight smile. "Thanks, Nora." She shook her head. "Don't worry. I'm not planning on a complete overhaul of my face. Hell, I might not get anything done at all. I'm just curious about my options."

The lights went down in the room, and everyone quieted as a live video feed appeared on the white screen. Mary Graves, said, "Ladies and Gentlemen, I give you Dr.

Corrine Sanduski, the foremost pioneer in beauty enhancement."

"Hello, everyone," the doctor said with enthusiasm. She stood next to another woman reclined and draped in an examination chair, one that looked more like the kind you'd find at a dentist than a doctor's office. "Welcome."

Mary clapped her hands, prompting the crowd to clap along with her. "Dr. Corrine will be giving you a live demonstration of the PDO threads to lift the jowls and plump the lips of our gracious volunteer, Tammilynn. Everyone give Tammilynn a big round of applause."

The audience clapped again.

The guinea pig smiled and waved.

Mary Graves continued, "While the demonstration is going on, you'll be able to see an immediate result. I'll take questions after Dr. Corrine is finished."

Pippa looked a little green.

"Are you okay?" I whispered.

She shook her head and clutched her belly. "My stomach is seriously messed up."

I hated seeing her suffer. I took Gilly's hand. "I'm going to take Pippa back to the room, then go and get her some Pepto from the gift shop."

Gilly nodded. "Go." She patted the top of my hand. "I'll take pictures and notes."

I was suddenly glad we were seated in the back. With the lights down and the video sound up, we barely drew any attention to ourselves as we made our way out the door and into the hall.

"Oh, God, Nora, I'm not going to make it," Pippa said

as we hurried through the vendor hall toward the elevators. She belched again then moaned. "We have to hurry."

"We are." I put my arm around her. "We'll make it."

Getting on the elevator brought little relief. We were on the third floor and had to get to the fourteenth, and it seemed as if the damn elevator was going to stop on every level to admit and discharge people.

Pippa whimpered.

"Come on, come on," I muttered. I was so stressed for Pip that I started to do a jittery dance as if I were the one who needed to use the bathroom. All the passengers had exited by the tenth floor, and we passed the eleventh floor without stopping. "Only three more floors," I told her. "Almost there."

The elevator doors opened on the twelfth floor. Pippa bit down on her lower lip as a man got on with us. My eyes widened. It was Brian Langford, the guy from Konash Technology. The guy Gregory had accused me of spying for.

"Hi," he said, giving me a nod.

I nodded back but didn't speak. I detected the unmistakable scent of eucalyptus and cedarwood as Langford turned his back to me to face the doors.

*"What is this?" a man asks, his voice full of accusation. "Are you recording me?"*

*"I don't know what you're talking about," a woman says. Her dark hair and voice tells me it's Samantha.*

*He grabs her pink tablet from the hotel desk. "I don't believe you."*

*The woman rushes over and tries to take the tablet away from the guy.*

*"Did you record us before? Are you trying to blackmail me?"*

*"Why would I do that?" She attempts to grab it again. "Give it to me. Give it back." Panic is shredding her voice. When she lunges, he swats her away, and she stumbles over to the bed. She fumbles to open the drawer of the nightstand, lifts up a Yellow Pages telephone book, and pulls out a pistol hiding underneath. Her hands are shaking, but she raises the gun and takes aim. "Put it down and get out of my room, Brian. Get out now."*

*The man raises one hand as he sets the tablet down.*

I put my hand over my mouth as the elevator opened to the fourteenth floor. Brian Langford moved to the side as I escorted Pippa out and down the hall toward our room.

"Cripes, Nora," she said. "You look almost as bad as I feel. What's wrong?"

"That was Langford, the guy who was fighting with Gregory."

"And?"

"And," I said. "I'm pretty sure he had a strong motive to want Samantha dead."

# CHAPTER 12

*I* picked up stomachache drugs and two big bottles of water from the hotel gift shop. After I got Pippa settled with meds and hydration, and tucked in for a nap, I left the hotel room and tracked down Gilly.

"So, you're telling me that this Langford character and the dead girl were lovers?" Gilly asked as we circled the Londa Angelista VIP Lounge. She had a massive goodie bag slung over her shoulder and was holding it down with her elbow as if someone might come along and try to snatch it from her.

"I think so," I said. "And he thought she was secretly recording their interactions."

"Audio or video?"

"I don't know. He asked if she was recording him, but there was nothing more specific in the memory."

"She had a gun?"

I nodded. "She'd kept it in her nightstand under a phone book."

"I wonder if the police found it. Do you think the police searched her room?"

"Doubtful." I shook my head. "If the police determine Samantha's death is an accident, then it's illegal for them to search her room. It will be up to the hotel to gather up all her belongings, catalog them, and get them sent to her family."

She picked up a shimmering coral lipstick from a sample basket and examined it carefully. "Maybe we should look for that security guy and ask him. I mean, it couldn't hurt."

"You mean Luscious Luke?" I grinned. "Good idea."

"Nora!" Blanche tapped me on the shoulder. "Are you enjoying yourself?"

"Hi," I said, startled to find her suddenly in front of me. Her pink hair was pinned back with a clip that spelled out, *Love*, in cursive. I elbowed my BFF. "Gilly, this is Blanche."

"Oh, hi!" Gilly impulsively embraced Blanche, who, luckily, didn't seem to mind one bit as she returned the squeeze. "Thank you so much." Gilly waggled her brows and tapped her Gold VIP badge.

"I was happy to do it," Blanche said. Unexpectedly, she pulled a soap out of her bag. It had a strip of paper wrapped on one side, and it was a decent version of my beach soap, one of the designs I'd demonstrated.

"That turned out great," I told her.

She lit up with joy. "Will you sign it for me? I still can't believe it's you. I've seen the ice cream cone soaps on your website, and I ordered them. Their fantastic, but I'd love to see how you made them. Do you think you could show that in your next demo series?"

"Uhm, maybe," I said, taking the soap and a pen she handed to me. I signed my name on the strip of paper.

"Thank you so much," she said, as she gently deposited the soap back in her bag. "That's going into my display at home."

"You got it to just the right cure, so make sure you wrap it in plastic, so it doesn't dry out any more than it has."

"That's a great tip." She bounced on her toes. "Thanks. Meeting you has been a highlight. I could tell by your videos that you were such a genuine person."

I laughed nervously. "Thank you." Blanche seemed harmless. Although her obsession with me and my soaps was a little strange, I liked her. And she'd done me a solid with the VIP upgrades. It was nice having someone on the inside of the convention. As an insider, had she heard anything about Samantha Jones' death? It wouldn't surprise me to find out that the hotel was keeping the incident hushed up. Even so, I figured there had to be a gossip mill with the convention workers and the hotel staff, and maybe Blanche might have heard a rumor or two about the incident.

"I heard the Selebrate launch might be canceled," I said casually. "Do you know why?"

Blanche's scandalized expression told me right away that she had juicy information. "Oh my gosh, I'm not sure I should say anything..." She leaned in closer and lowered her voice. "Apparently, some bigwig's assistant was found in the pod's display room yesterday." Her eyes widened as she added, "She. Was. Dead."

"Do you know how she died?" asked Gilly.

"I was told she'd suffocated. An allergy to a chemical or something." She absently touched her neck. "Anyhow, Selebrate is still planning to go ahead with the party."

"In the same room?" Gilly's lower lip curled. "Yuck."

"No, of course not," corrected Blanche. "That would be..." She shivered. "The entire staff was in a tizzy this morning, working to move the party to the Tulip Ballroom."

"One of their employees dies, and they decide to have the party anyway," I said. "That seems morbid."

"Poor Samantha hasn't even been dead for twenty-four hours, and they're just moving right along like she didn't die horribly," said Gilly. Gilly's expression held the same repulsion that churned in my gut.

I glanced at Blanche and saw her amazed expression. "How do you know that?" she asked.

"We...uh, sorta found her," I admitted.

"Oh, my gosh. You guys must've been horrified," Blanche said.

"It was terrible," Gilly agreed. Then she went one step further than I'd wanted. "Nora is an investigator. She's helped our local police solve two major crimes."

"Really?" Blanche blinked at me. "I thought you made soaps."

"That's my full-time job," I affirmed. "But Gilly is right, I do help the police from time to time. I have," I didn't want to tell her about my psychic nose. For one, it was hard to believe, and for two, it was a weird thing to tell a mostly stranger. So, I kept it vague, "an ability to see things that other people might not be able to pick up on." There. Not a lie, but not the whole truth.

"Like Sherlock Holmes?"

"Something like that." Only nothing like that. Although I was reasonably observant, thanks to my upbringing. "And my father was a police officer, an investigator for most of his career. He taught me a lot about how to work a crime scene."

"So, it was a crime?" she hissed. "Do you think a murderer is walking around this conference?"

"We don't know how the woman died," I admitted. "So, there's a possibility it could have been some kind of horrible accident." Though, I had serious doubts.

"Are you guys going to the launch?" Blanche asked.

"Yes," I replied. "I'll admit I'm more than a little curious about the Stress-less pod."

"Well, if you need anything." The younger woman put her hand on my forearm for emphasis. "Anything at all. You got my number."

"Thank you." I tipped my head to her. "I will take you up on that offer."

After Blanche departed, Gilly said, "Maybe we shouldn't have told Blanche about our part in finding the body."

"Blanche is someone who can move around this convention without drawing too much attention to herself. An extra pair of eyes and ears, if we need them, can't hurt."

"Young eyes," Gilly added. "And young ears."

"My ears are just fine," I grumbled as I touched my

earlobe. I couldn't believe Gregory was going ahead with the launch. If something in that machine was the cause of Samantha's death, why would he chance using it on someone else? Unless he knew precisely what killed his assistant and was confident it wouldn't happen again. "I need to find Gregory."

"Are you sure that's a good idea?" Gilly asked. She threw a few foundation samples into her bag. "He was pretty volatile last night."

"I need to ask him why this launch is so important. Important enough that he won't cancel after his assistant died in the damn contraption."

Gilly nodded. "Okay. Let's do it."

* * *

A CHILL RAN through me as we exited the elevator onto the sixth floor. The hall was eerily quiet, and there was a velvet rope cordoning off the area. A big sign said, *No Admittance. Selebrate Stress-less Demo will open at 6:30 p.m. Location has moved to the Tulip Ballroom.*

"There's nobody up here," Gilly said.

I sighed. "It was a long shot."

"Do you want to sneak past the rope?"

"I do," I said on a laugh. "But we probably shouldn't."

"You think we might find another body."

"Lord, I hope not." My phone buzzed in my purse. "Hold on." I dug it out. "It's Pippa. She says she's feeling a little better, but to go to lunch without her."

"Poor thing. Well, I'm glad she's feeling better." Gilly's face brightened. "So, where do we want to get lunch?"

"What are you all doing up here?" Luke Robson walked up the hallway toward us.

I half-smiled as Gilly straightened her top and fluffed her curls forward over her shoulders at his approach.

"You look great," I said out the side of my mouth. I glanced up at Robson. He struck me as the kind of guy who would smell bullshit a mile away, and since there wasn't any good reason to keep the truth from him, I said, "We were looking for Gregory Paramount."

"Mr. Paramount left for lunch about ten minutes ago," he said. "I heard him say he was going to Darbie's, here in the hotel."

His hands were down by his sides. He had neatly trimmed nails, but not a professional manicure, but more importantly, he didn't have a wedding ring on. Of course, some men didn't wear wedding rings, so I wouldn't assume anything. Still, I felt like I had to keep an eye out for my BFF. She wasn't exactly well known for being attracted to decent men. It made me wonder if Luke had some skeletons in his closet.

"Thanks for the information."

"It doesn't cost me anything. It's not like it's classified." He turned his attention to Gilly. "Hello, Ms. Martin."

"Hello, Mr. Robson."

"You can just call me Luke."

"Then you have to call me Gilly," she said coyly. Her eyelashes fluttered in a way that looked flirty and cute. If I had tried the same maneuver, I would have looked like I was having a seizure.

I could tell by the look of adoration on Robson's face

that the batting of the lashes had the desired effect. The corner of his mouth crooked up. His smile was charming. "Okay, Gilly." He said her name as if he was testing it on his lips. "It's nice to see you again."

Gilly blushed just the right amount. "And under better circumstances," Gilly said before she sobered her gaze and segued into the question I wanted. "Have you heard anything about how Samantha Jones died?"

"Actually, I have. The medical examiner suspects tetrodotoxin."

"You mean, like the stuff that's in that pufferfish?"

"Fugu, to be precise. She and a few friends went to a specialty tasting at the Wasabi Sushi Ai at the Marlon Hotel across the street for lunch. The ME says the symptoms are consistent with eating contaminated fish. The health department has shut the restaurant down to investigate." He shook his head. "Damn, who in their right mind eats fugu?"

"I heard it's delicious," Gilly said.

Both Robson and I made a "yuck" face.

Anyhow," he continued, "They finished the autopsy this morning. Preliminary results indicate Ms. Jones had a reaction consistent with the toxin. It paralyzed her lungs and throat, and she suffocated. But the toxicology report won't be back for a few weeks. However, based on the ME's report, the coroner is calling it an accidental death."

"Cripes, what a way to die." Still, I had a feeling there was something sinister about Samantha's death. "Were there any signs of a struggle?"

He gave me a flat look. "According to the medical

examiner, there were no signs of a struggle—clean finger-nails, no unusual bruises, and so forth."

"No needle marks?" I asked. Could Samantha's death and all the chaos surrounding Selebrate and their launch party be a mere coincidence? Yes, I thought, but I still didn't think so."

"None that I was told about." Luke frowned. "Is there a reason you think Ms. Jones' death is not accidental?"

Aside from the scent-inspired memories, I didn't have anything at all to prove my growing suspicion about Samantha's death.

"What about her room? Has anyone searched it yet?" What I really wanted to know is if Robson had found her gun or her tablet?

"Not yet," he answered with a scant of suspicion. "I'm getting ready to go up there for a preliminary walk-through."

Before I could ask the impossible, Gilly beat me to it. "I don't suppose we could," she shrugged, "go up to her room with you?"

"You're cute," Robson said. "But that's not going to happen."

We got on the elevator after Robson. He crossed his arm over his chest. "Uh-uh. This isn't happening."

Gilly did not back down. "We're not following you. We just happen to be going the same way."

"Pure coincidence," I agreed without any real convic-tion. "We have a thing on," I peered at the panel and squinted at the lit number, "the twelfth floor."

A slow smile spread on his lips. When we reached the twelfth floor, Gilly and I exited ahead of him, but sly

Luke Robson didn't follow us out. We turned around in time to see him casually wave goodbye as the doors closed between us.

"That sneaky bastard," Gilly said with a grin. "Is it sad that I think he's even hotter now?"

"Pay attention to the numbers to see what floor he gets off on." I pushed the up button, and the light came on.

"In my estimation, he could totally get off on the fourteenth floor."

"I don't need to hear that." I laughed.

"Says the woman having phone sex in the middle of the night in our hotel room."

"In my defense..." I shrugged.

Gilly laughed. "That's it? That's your defense?"

"It's all I got." She stood beside me as we watched the light stop on the eighteenth floor, and the car headed back down. "Here we go," I said.

"What if he got off on the seventeenth floor? It was lit up for a hard second."

"Okay, you take the seventeenth, and I'll search the eighteenth. Whoever finds your Luscious Luke first texts the other."

Gilly nodded. "It's a plan." The doors opened, and we got on. "The hunt for Luke Robson is on."

# CHAPTER 13

The design for the hotel was basically a square pattern, so I took the first right when I hit the hall. I discovered right away that this floor was nearly identical to my own, so I gave the ice machine alcove a wide berth, just in case.

I couldn't shake the feeling that Samantha's death was not accidental, even with the evidence that she might have eaten bad sushi. Still, I only had my gut as evidence.

I didn't know enough about tetrodotoxin poisoning to know how quickly the symptoms came on. Even so, I couldn't help thinking that Samantha would have been feeling sick or something when she got to the display room. Was that why she'd been inside the pod? Had she started to feel bad after lunch, so she'd wanted to rest?

I cycled through the few things I did know. Remy Tarlington was angry about having her work stolen, as she'd put it. Gregory was upset because his prize new toy had been tampered with. Brian Langford thought she wanted to blackmail him. She was found dead in the meditation pod.

Before I could ponder more, I saw Robson standing outside a room at the end of the third hall. I shot off a quick text to Gilly before I reached him. He appeared to be examining something, and I was surprised to see him wearing gloves.

"What's wrong?" I asked.

He whipped around to face me, his hand going to his side as if ready to draw a weapon. When his gaze fell on me, his shoulders relaxed. "I told you that you can't be here."

"Yet, here I am," I said. "You look worried. Did something happen?" Maybe he saw the pistol.

"I haven't even been inside the room."

I balled my fist onto my hip and stretched to peer around him. All I saw was the door. Nothing more. "What are you waiting for?"

Robson sighed then studied me for a moment as if trying to make up his mind about me. Finally, he said, "I guess it doesn't hurt to tell you." He stepped out of the way and showed me a piece of tape stretching from the door to the wall.

"What am I looking at?"

"I taped this yesterday after the police arrived. I gave orders that no one was allowed in this room until the investigation was over."

"But?"

"But...someone replaced the tape I put on here."

I narrowed my gaze. "Is it a different brand or something?"

Robson shook his head, his hazel-gray eyes clouded with worry. "It's the hotel tape."

"Then how do you know it's been tampered with?"

"I dog-ear my tape and make a date mark on the inside of the ear. It's a habit from my military days."

I examined the tape. All four corners were flat. "Are you sure?"

Robson nodded. "I'm positive. But the person who removed and replaced it obviously didn't know. They replicated size and placement almost exactly. Whoever it was didn't want anyone knowing they were here."

"We should go inside."

He gave me a "yeah, right" stare. "We," he gestured between us with a finger, "won't be going anywhere."

"Did I miss anything?" Gilly asked as she came up the hallway.

Robson pulled his shoulders back and shifted his stance. His tone changed to something a little more genial. "You're just in time to take your friend back downstairs."

"Well, that doesn't sound right," Gilly said. "Especially when we really want to be on this floor right now."

"Yes, we," I emphasized "we" the same way he had, with a finger gesture back and forth between Gilly and me, "don't want to go back downstairs."

"I can have you thrown out of the hotel," he bantered.

"But you won't, will you?" Gilly asked.

He looked at her for a moment then shook his head. "No. I won't. But you two have to stay out in the hall-way." He turned around and produced a utility knife. He slid the blade forward and made a neat incision through the tape where it connected the door and the frame. He retracted the blade and put it back in his pocket, then produced a black card. He dropped it into the lock and turned the handle when the light went from red to green.

He stretched his hand back, motioning for Gilly and me to stay out of the way as he quietly cracked the door open.

"There's no one in the room," I said.

"How could you know that?" he whispered. "Are you a psychic?"

I laughed because, yes, I was, sort of, but it wasn't the reason I knew no one was in the room. "You can't re-tape a door on the outside from the inside."

His cheeks flushed, and he sheepishly grinned. "I suppose you're right." He glanced at Gilly. "I'm having an off day, and you all are a distraction." He pushed the door open and quickly went inside, the door closing behind him. I'd only gotten a glimmer of an open suitcase on one of those fold-out holders.

"Damn it. I couldn't get a good look."

Gilly nudged me after he went inside. She spoke quietly. "What did I miss?"

I matched her quieter tone. "Someone changed the tape on the outside of the door, and your future husband thinks someone entered illegally."

She elbowed me harder. "Stop that. I am not getting married again, like ever."

"You say that now," I teased, moving out of the way when she came back in for another rib grazer.

"Why don't you tell him about Gregory?" she whispered. "You wouldn't have had that smell-o-rama vision if he hadn't been in the room."

"You're right. But how am I supposed to explain how I know?" I asked. "It's not like I can tell him about my nosey nose."

"Why not? I mean, the worse that can happen is he'll think you're a kook."

"Or he'll think I'm involved," I hissed. "That could be worse."

She shrugged and nodded. "There's that. But where's your motive? Besides, it's not like you force-fed her the fugu."

"If that's even how she died."

"You don't buy it?"

"Maybe. I could be Don Quixote tilting at windmills."

"I'm a believer, Nora. If your instinct tells you there's more to Samantha's death, then we can't just leave it alone. Her loved ones deserve to know the truth, whatever it might be. Accidental or otherwise."

"Agreed." But where could we even start? If the police weren't going to investigate, and the only evidence I had was a handful of disjointed memories and a few arguments, along with a gut feeling. "It doesn't make a whiff of sense."

Gilly smirked. "A whiff of sense, huh?"

"You know what I mean." I cracked a smile then frowned. A woman was dead. The woman who'd been in this room. I knocked on the door. "Did you find anything, Mr. Robson?"

He came to the door and opened it barely wide enough to fit his head. His gaze narrowed on me. "Why are you two still here? You should go and enjoy your conference."

I ignored his dismissal. "Did you find a pink tablet in her room? Or a gun?"

"Why would there be a gun in Ms. Jones' room?" he asked. He gave me a shrewd stare. "What aren't you telling me, Ms. Black? Do you know something about her death that you didn't tell the police?"

Yes, I screamed on the inside. Brian Langford had threatened Samantha, and she had pulled a gun on him. When she'd retrieved it, it had been in the nightstand and hidden under a telephone directory. "Did you check inside the bedside table? It might be under the telephone book."

He frowned. "Don't go anywhere."

"You couldn't get rid of us if you tried," Gilly said.

This caused Robson to shake his head, but I saw the smile peeking at the corners.

I rolled my eyes. "I should just leave this alone."

"Right, Nora. You're so good a leaving stuff alone." Gilly put her arm around my shoulder. "Look, I know you were excited about coming to the conference and seeing old friends and all. But the only time I see you this... excited is when you're with Ezra Holden or you're solving a puzzle of some kind."

"You mean when I'm investigating."

"I didn't want to say it that way, but yes. You have a way of getting to the core of a matter."

"Since my near-death incident."

"Since your whole life." Gilly gave me a squeeze. "Do

you remember when your dad was trying to track down that ring of car thieves?"

I smiled. "When we were sophomores."

"Yes. You straight-up Nancy Drewed that mystery and gave your dad the information he needed to take down Mr. Donell."

"That gaslighting son-of-a-jerk was failing me in shop class. I still can't believe he was using teenage boys to steal cars then cut them up, right under the nose of the school." Really, if it hadn't been for Brett Peters, a bad boy with a crush on me, that case could have gone on for a lot longer. "He would have gotten away with it too."

Gilly leaned in. "If it hadn't been for that meddling kid."

We giggled. I hated to admit it, but she was right. One of the things I'd missed about being married to Shawn, the current chief of police in Garden Cove, was him coming home and talking out his cases with me. He'd relied on my intuition. I thought of our early years fondly. Shawn was a good man, and at one time, we'd wanted the same things. Or so I'd thought.

Now I had Ezra in my life, and he, like Shawn, told me about his cases and valued my input, above and beyond my newfound aroma mojo. Only, Shawn had wanted my involvement on his terms, while Ezra didn't try to keep me in a box.

The room door opened back up. Robson looked at me without any hint of amusement in his constipated expression. "How did you know?"

"You found the gun?"

"I found a 9mm pistol under a phone book and at the

back of the drawer. If you hadn't told me to look there, I probably would have missed it. So, tell me how you knew?"

"Would you believe it was a good guess?" I asked.

"No," he said. "I would not believe you. Not at all."

I wished I could come up with a great Sherlock Holmes reveal, like I saw a callus on her trigger finger, along with ink stains from the yellow pages, so I deduced it was in the nightstand. But I figured he would believe that about as much as he would believe I could see people's memories when I smelled a scent that had strong emotions attached to it.

"Well," he said, tapping his foot and clearly agitated. "I can only think of one reason you would know where the gun was located." He pointed at me. "You're the one who entered this room illegally."

"I didn't go into Samantha Jones' room," I denied.

"I'm afraid I'm going to have to take you down to my office for questioning, Ms. Black."

"Luke," Gilly demanded. "No."

"Tell me how you knew about the gun?"

"Lucky guess," I said, knowing that wouldn't be enough for someone who used to be an investigator, but I could hope.

He frowned, the lines in his forehead deepening to canyons. "If you went into Ms. Jones' room and went through her belongings, it's against the law."

"I didn't. But I don't have a good answer for you about how I knew the gun would be there."

His expression was pained. "Then you leave me no choice. I'm going to need you to come with me."

"This is a bunch of crap," Gilly said. "Nora hasn't been anywhere near here."

"I have to do my job." He gave me a pleading look. "Please don't make me handcuff you."

The blood drained from my face. "I'll go without a fuss, but you're making a mistake."

Robson got on his radio. "Raul."

"Yeah, Luke," came a voice over the speaker.

"I need you to drop what you're doing, grab a kit from the office, and come stand guard over Room 1856."

"Don't do this, Luke. You're making a mistake," Gilly pleaded. "Nora, tell him."

I shook my head. The truth was unbelievable. I needed someone who knew me, who knew my worth, but also had authority and could testify to my weird ability. Gilly and Pippa didn't have the gravitas of another officer. I needed...

I locked gazes with Gilly. "Call Ezra."

# CHAPTER 14

"*I* don't know how many times I have to tell you I didn't go into Samantha's room." I'd sat in the security office for the past hour and a half while Robson had gone back up to the dead woman's room to search it more thoroughly. For the past ten minutes, he'd been interrogating me as if I were a criminal. Dad used to tease me about ending up on the wrong side of the law. Ah, if he could see me now. "Where is Gilly?"

Robson sat behind a cold gray metal desk in a functional office chair. He had put me in a non-rolling chair on the other side. The security office had gray walls, which should have made the room feel lifeless, but the dark blue trim added some warmth.

"Your friend is waiting out in the lobby." He rubbed his hand over his head. His desk had a computer monitor and an ergonomic keyboard pushed to one side. The computer itself had to be under the desk, but because I hadn't heard the fans, and the monitor looked like a dinosaur, I didn't think it was turned on. It wasn't surprising. Robson held a yellow legal pad and a pencil—totally old school—for taking notes.

"I don't think your friend is too fond of me." He set down his pad and pencil. "If looks could kill, she'd be my prime suspect."

"Her looks can be withering, but I've never known them to be lethal," I told him. Gilly had thought Robson was handsome, but he wasn't wrong. She would have my back in this and all matters. Sisters before misters. Still, I didn't think Robson was a bad guy.

I wondered if Gilly had gotten in touch with Ezra. I felt foolish now, telling Gilly to call him as if I needed rescuing. I didn't. At least, I hoped not. Still, it said something about the depth of my feelings for Ezra that in my moment of trouble, he was the first person I'd thought of.

Robson stood up and walked around the desk. "We could end this right now, and you could go back to your weekend of beauty and whatever it is you all do at these conventions. Just answer my one simple question." He walked over to the wall and leaned against a tall black file cabinet. "How did you know about the gun in the nightstand?"

Shows what he knew. There was nothing simple about the question or the answer. "Dude, think about it." I tapped my temple for emphasis. "If I had known where Samantha Jones' room was located, I wouldn't have gotten off on the twelfth floor when you tricked us."

A look of consternation wrinkled Robson's brow. "Or," he countered, "you knew what I would find, so you pretended to be tricked." His frown deepened. "I really don't know what to make of you."

"Look, I have sort of a sixth sense." Only really, it was one of the five senses supernaturally enhance, but I wasn't ready to divulge that information. "I've helped the police out before with investigations. You can call the Garden Cove PD." And, if Ezra was on his way, Robson would have the news right from the detective's mouth.

The ex-military cop didn't try to hide his incredulity. "I mean this most respectfully because you seem like a nice person, but why in the world would the police let you investigate a misdemeanor jaywalking, let alone a major crime?"

"I *am* a nice person," I said. I chose my next words carefully. "I have a certain specialty. I can tell things about people and situations..." How was I going to put this? "From odors. I have a highly developed sense of smell."

"Please don't yank my chain, Ms. Black. I've seen the TV series with the detective who walks into a murder scene and knows who did it by the scent of mustard on the floor next to the victim. But this is real life, and it's serious business. If you can't give me some answers. Real answers..." His gaze narrowed on me. "Or I'm going to have to call the police to investigate you for a breaking-and-entering charge. I don't want to have to do that to you."

I sighed and worked super hard not to roll my eyes. Because a) I tried really hard not to disrespect people for doing their jobs, and b) I didn't want him calling the police. Once they got involved, I would end up down at the station and not in the hotel, where I needed to be if I wanted to figure out what happened to Samantha.

"Go ahead and call the police," I said. "But it'll be a

big waste of everyone's time. I wouldn't break into some-one's room and search through their belongings. Espe-cially after that someone died."

I understood how my knowledge of the weapon could be tough to swallow. Robson didn't know me from Adam, and he had no reason to believe me. Why had I even mentioned the gun in the first place? Because I was an idiot, that's why.

I leaned forward in the seat and placed my palms on my knees. "Look. Until I followed you to the eighteenth floor, I'd never been above fourteen, which is where my suite is located. Don't you have cameras on the elevators? You can check out the footage and see I'm telling the truth."

He nodded. "We do, but you could have taken the stairs to avoid the cameras."

I nearly choked on a laugh. "Mr. Robson, I have bum knees. While it might be possible to walk up all of them, coming back down would be a real pain. Literally."

Robson loosened his collar, then took off his jacket and laid it on the back of his chair. He paced in front of me. "Are you like a mentalist?"

He wasn't far off the mark. Most pretend psychics were mentalists, people with high observation skills able to draw reliable conclusions from the minutest of details. I liked to think of myself as someone who noticed a lot of things, but I wasn't good enough to con someone into believing I was psychic. If I wanted Robson to believe me, I'd have to prove that I had seen the gun without physi-cally being in the room.

I scanned the office, looking for anything that might

have a scent. The desk and bookshelves contained stacks of paperwork, procedure books, and other security stuff, but nothing personal, and certainly nothing that had a smell that I might be able to read.

"I'm not a mentalist." I shook out my hands. "I have other...gifts."

"Like what?"

I would have liked nothing better than to give him a demonstration, but there was nothing to scent here. "Are there any smells that mean something to you?"

His nose scrunched up. "That's an oddly personal question."

"Don't you have anything in this office that means anything to you?" I sighed hard as I looked around. "I mean, this place doesn't have anything personal in it. What are you, a robot?"

"This is my workspace. Not my personal space." He narrowed his gaze at me. "You're a strange one, aren't you?"

"Strange is appropriate. So, tell me a scent or fragrance that brings back memories for you."

"Why? What can this possibly have to do with Samantha Jones?"

"If you'll just indulge me for one minute, I will demonstrate the why."

"Fine," Robson said. He scratched the back of his head, his gaze drifting as if deep in thought. When he glanced back at me, his eyes were sparkling with something akin to mischief. "I've got it."

When he didn't say more, I said, "This isn't a magic trick where you don't show me your card. You have to actually tell me what the scent is. Just don't tell me the memory you associate with it."

"Okay." He pursed his lips. "The smell of Tabasco."

A weird choice. I hoped it was not something kinky, like he liked to drip hot sauce on his lovers or something, because that was not a memory I wanted to experience. "Is there anywhere around here to find some Tabasco?"

He frowned. "Where is this leading?"

"I have to actually smell it. I told you, it's my nose that has the talent." I touched the tip of my nose for emphasis. "If finding Tabasco is too hard, pick something else. But the aroma has to be something you feel a strong emotional connection about."

Robson looked doubtful, but he turned and opened the top drawer of his file cabinet and pulled out a lunchbox. He opened it up and extracted what looked like a kid-sized bottle of Tabasco and handed it to me unopened.

"This is adorable," I said. "I didn't know it came in a fun size." I suddenly felt vulnerable and nervous. The memories were trance-like at times, and I wanted my BFF in the room just in case I needed her support. I glanced up at Robson. "Can Gilly come in for this?"

"Is she part of the gag?"

"There is no gag." I crossed my heart. "I'm not trying to con you. I'd just feel better if Gilly was in here with me."

Robson crossed the small room to the door, opened it up, and said, "Raul, bring Ms. Black's friend in."

"Which one?" I heard him ask.

"Are there more than one?"

"There's a Gillian Martin, Pippa Davenport, Jordy Hines, and Ezra Holden."

My chest squeezed as my heart picked up the pace. Ezra was already here. Dang, Ezra had made spectacular time. He must have dropped everything, and he brought Jordy along as well. I couldn't help myself. I smiled.

Robson looked at me. "I guess you know all the names."

I nodded. "Yes. Those are my friends. Ezra Holden is a special investigator for the Garden Cove PD. I have worked with him on two murder cases." I turned the Tabasco bottle between my fingers. "I don't suppose you'll let them all in the room?"

"I want answers, Ms. Black."

"And if you bring my friends back, I promise, I will tell you everything."

I just hoped that when I opened this bottle of hot sauce and took a sniff, it would reveal enough of Robson's past to make him believe in my psychic nose.

Robson opened the door wider. "Send them all back," he said.

"You sure, Luke?" Raul asked.

"Nope," Robson replied. "But do it anyway."

# CHAPTER 15

he office space diminished in size as the room filled up with my nearest and dearest. Gilly and Pippa came through first, both looking ready to fight.

I mouthed, "How are you feeling?" to Pippa and rubbed my tummy.

She nodded and mouthed back, "Better."

Jordy, who had his long hair pulled back in a Viking-style braid, walked in behind Pippa and stayed at her back. I had a suspicion that if she or Gilly had decided to jump Robson, he would have joined them in the ass-kicking. Ezra, who was the opposite of Jordy—clean-cut, no beard or tattoos that could be seen—looked like he could spit nails as he strolled through the open door. My body buzzed at the sight of him.

He glanced over to me, and I gave him a pleased smile. The circumstances were awful, but I was always glad to see him. "You got here quick."

"Of course I did." He walked over to me and tilted my chin up. "Are you okay?"

"Fine," I said. "This is all just a big misunderstanding."

Ezra turned my wrists over. I showed him the Tabasco bottle. "What's this for?"

"A demonstration," I said cryptically.

Robson cleared his throat to get our attention. "I'll need all of you to quiet down so that Ms. Black can finally tell me the truth."

Ezra took his wallet out of the back pocket of his jeans and showed Robson his credentials. "Detective Ezra Holden. Garden Cove PD. Special investigations," he said.

"Luke Robson," Robson replied. "Twenty years of criminal investigation with the Army's CID."

That's where the niceties ended as Ezra gave him a ten-mile stare. "Mr. Robson, why are you treating Nora like a criminal suspect?"

Robson looked as if he was going to challenge Ezra but then shook his head. "There was a gun in a dead woman's room, and Ms. Black knew it was in there and exactly where to find it. On top of that, someone had broken into the room and replaced the tape to make the room appear undisturbed. You can see how this could be construed as suspicious."

Ezra glanced at me. I raised my brows then touched my nose. He sighed. Heavily. He nodded to Robson. "The police are saying the death is accidental. She had a reaction to bad sushi."

"Is there any good sushi?" Jordy muttered. Pippa smiled and shook her head.

Robson cocked his head sideways. "You called the precinct?"

Ezra's expression was hard. "I know a guy."

"That doesn't make it legal to break into a deceased person's hotel room." Robson sounded exasperated. "I'm about two ticks from kicking all of you out so I can finish my chat with Ms. Black. The only reason you're in here is she promised me some answers if I let you come back."

Raul hovered in the entrance. "You need me, Luke?"

Robson looked at all of us and said, "I don't know. Do I need Raul to stay?"

I stood up and shook my head. "I'd prefer not to say what I have to say or do what I have to do to prove my innocence with Raul in the room." I looked at the big burly guard. "No offense."

He shrugged. "I'm not offended."

"Nora," Ezra said cautiously. "Are you sure you want to do this?"

I held up the Tabasco bottle and unscrewed the lid. "In for a penny, in for a pound."

Robson gave me a skeptical look, but told Raul, "It's fine. Close the door behind you."

"You're the boss," the big man said then left.

Robson stared at me. "Well, go on," he said. "Show me your hoodoo."

"One hoodoo, coming right up." I held the bottle up and inhaled. The pungent aroma of spicy aged peppers and vinegar tickled my nose. I sneezed, but no vision came. I looked at Robson. "Are you sure this stuff means something to you?"

He nodded his affirmative.

Maybe because it had been an unopened bottle, it didn't have a scent memory attached to it yet. I turned my left hand over and poured some of the hot sauce on the back of my hand. "Can you come over and smell this?"

Robson snorted a laugh. "You're kidding, right?"

"Nope," I said. "Can you humor me?"

"I have been humoring you," he replied.

"Just do it, for heaven's sake," Gilly demanded.

Robson grimaced. With a fair amount of frustration, he added, "Fine," before stalking over to me. He dipped his head and sniffed and straightened. "Yep," he said, "smells like Tabasco."

I crossed my metaphorical fingers and toes that my ability would work.

"Maybe you should sit down for this," Pippa said to me. "That last one nearly took it out of you."

I wanted to argue, but she wasn't wrong. The vision I'd had when Gregory had confronted me in the hall the night before had left me lightheaded and weak. I sat back down. Slowly, hoping like hell I'd get some kind of reading, I raised the back of my hand to my nose.

*My senses reel with the scent of Tabasco, along with the acrid smell of wood smoke. Four men are sitting around a campfire. They are wearing camouflage uniforms and billed caps that match. I can't see their faces, but I can read their names above their left upper pockets.*

*Leary, Thompson, Jenkins, and Robson.*

*"Christ, my feet feel like they're never going to dry out," Leary says. "I can't believe we marched fifteen miles with sixty pounds of gear on our back."*

*"In the damn rain," Jenkins adds. "My blisters have blisters."*

*The men laugh. The camaraderie is palpable.*

*"Let's chow and get some rest," Robson says. He sounds different than he does now. Younger.*

*They tear open brown plastic bags that say MRE. Robson's says beef stew on the packaging, and Jenkins' is chicken chow mein. Jenkins and Robson pull out tiny bottles of Tabasco sauce from inside the bags.*

*"Gross," Leary says. "I don't know how you can eat that stuff."*

*Both Jenkins and Robson say, "It covers the taste." They elbow each other and share another laugh. Even though the memory is fond, I can't shake an overwhelming sadness.*

I blinked as the security office reappeared. Then the scent of Tabasco took me in again.

*This time I am in a graveyard. A man stands in front of a grave. The headstone reads, "Michael C. Jenkins, Son, Husband, Father, and Friend. May 17, 1976 - August 8, 2005."*

*Cripes. Today is the fifteenth anniversary of Jenkins' death.*

*For several seconds, he just stands there over the grave of his friend. "Sorry, Mike, I got here as soon as I could," he says. "I was TDY in Germany when Dee called me. She and the kids are doing okay. I won't forget my promise to look in on them from time to time." He reaches into his pocket and pulls out a small bottle of Tabasco and sets it on the ledge of the base. "I know you'll want this when you get to where you're going." He pats the stone. "Just in case the food tastes bad."*

I breathed out a sigh of heartache and loss as the security office, my friends, and Robson all came back into view. This vision had been swampy with emotions that brought up fresh and unexpected grief for my mother.

I glanced at Ezra, struggling to hold back the tears.

"What's wrong?" he asked, his voice full of concern. "What did you see?"

I couldn't bring myself to speak it, and when my gaze shifted to Robson, I couldn't stop the choking sob.

"What's happening?" Robson asked. "Does she need a doctor?"

I took several deep breaths and took a tissue that Gilly had retrieved from her purse to wipe my eyes and blow my nose. "I'm so sorry," I said.

"Don't be sorry. Just tell me what's going on?"

I still lacked the control to convey what I'd seen, so I looked to Ezra for help.

He reached down and took my hand. "Nora sees memories," Ezra explained. "Other people's memories when they are tied to scent. What she saw from you must have been powerful."

Robson's eyes widened, stunned by Ezra's words. Then his face pinched with anger. "Nice try. I'm going to need better than some hokum story."

I inhaled sharply, and in one breath, blurted, "Michael C. Jenkins. August 8, 2005. Tabasco hides the taste."

Robson went completely pale. He staggered back and clutched his desktop to brace himself up. Gilly ran around his desk, got his chair, and pushed it around to him. "Here," she ordered him. "Sit down before you pass out."

"I'm so very, very sorry for your loss," I apologized. I hated that I'd invaded his private anguish, but he'd been the one to pick the Tabasco, not me. Of course, he probably hadn't expected anything would come of it.

"How could you know that?" he finally asked. He glared at Ezra. "Did you do a background check on me?"

"Even if I did, it's not like that bit of info would have popped up," Ezra said civilly. He didn't want to rub salt in the man's wound. He had compassion, and I loved that quality in him. "Nora saw the memory."

Robson shook his head, still struggling with disbelief.

"Leary, Jenkins, Thompson, and you were sitting around a campfire after a fifteen-mile march in the rain. You were getting ready to eat dinner from a brown plastic bag. Beef stew, and you and Jenkins both liked Tabasco because it covered the taste of the MRE food."

"MRE?" Pippa asked.

"Meal Ready-To-Eat. That was on our ruck march during basic training. Jenkins and I had joined the army together," Robson said, his voice loud and sharp. "Christ. I can't... How is this even possible?"

"I don't know how to explain it," I told him. "I had surgery in January, and I flatlined for less than half a minute. It's the only thing I can think of that makes any sense, that somehow, my near-death experience gave me the ability. The first time I saw someone else's memory was when I was in the recovery room."

"So, you just smell something, and you get a memory hit?"

"Not always. Like I said, the scent has to be tied to emotional memories. That's why I needed you to smell the Tabasco sauce. It was an unopened bottle, so it wasn't tied to any memories, yet. Not until you anchored it."

"And that's how you knew about the gun," he said, some of the color returning to his cheeks. Gilly placed her hand on his shoulder in a gesture of compassion. Robson didn't pull away.

"Yes," I confirmed. "I saw a memory of Samantha Jones arguing with Brian Langford in her hotel room. He thought she was recording them together, possibly for blackmail. He tried to take her tablet, and when he wouldn't give it back, she got the gun from the nightstand and pulled it on him."

"Then what happened?"

I shrugged. "I don't know. That was the end of the memory." I tugged at my chin. "Only..."

"Only what?"

"Only, the person who had the scent on them wasn't in the room when the memory occurred. I hadn't been sure what to make of it, but now I think it's because the scent wasn't tied to a memory for him, it was tied to Samantha Jones. I think I know who entered the room illegally."

Robson perked up. "Who?"

"Gregory. I think he was looking for Samantha's tablet."

"Do you think he might be involved in her demise?"

I shrugged. "Honestly, I don't know. But I find death by pufferfish highly suspect. I think it warrants further investigation."

Robson nodded. "It will take more evidence than this..." He waved his hand in a circle as if trying to figure out what to call my ability. My BFFs helped him out.

"Smell-o-vision," Gilly supplied.

"Aroma-mojo," Pippa added helpfully.

I pursed my lips and raised my brows at them. They both gave me a quick curtsy.

Robson shook his head. "I'll have to investigate in-house. And we have to be discreet. The last thing the hotel manager will want is for me to turn a probable acci-dent into a homicide."

"We can help," Gilly said.

Robson patted her hand, but he looked at me. "I have a feeling even if I say no, you're going to poke your nose around anyway."

"Smart man," Gilly said. "There might be some hope for you yet."

# CHAPTER 16

"*D*o you think they have rooms for you and Jordy?" I asked as the five of us—me, Ezra, Gilly, Pippa, and Jordy—crossed the lobby. Gilly had hung behind for a few seconds to have a quiet word with Robson but caught up to us before we'd gotten down the main hall.

"Jordy and I can share a room if we have to," Ezra said. "We talked about it on the way up. That way, we don't interrupt any of your plans."

Gilly piped up. "A dead body already did that. We missed our massages and our fancy dinner last night already." Gilly put her arm around my shoulder. "Come on. We should see if they have any extra rooms for the guys."

I was pretty good at reading my friend, and her body language told me she didn't mind if Ezra and Jordy stayed. "What are you up to?"

She smiled and tilted her head back and forth. "Nothing you need to worry about."

I glanced over at Pippa, who was smiling and happily holding Jordy's hand. Aaron Keller never stood a chance. "Are you good with that, Pippa? These guys sharing a room?"

"Fine by me," she said. "Let's just hope they have some available. The hotel has been booked for six months."

Samantha Jones' room would be available, but there was probably a waiting list.

"What about the Marlon, across the street?" Ezra said. "Jordy and I could go over there. It will give me a chance to check out the Wasabi Sushi Ai. I mean, they couldn't stay in business if they were poisoning guests every week."

Jordy agreed. "And it's close enough for us to come back over at a moment's notice."

I smiled up at Ezra. "You must have broken speed records to get here as fast as you did. And you had time to pick up Jordy." I shook my head. "I'm impressed."

Jordy laughed. "Don't be too impressed. He was at the cafe having a coffee and a scone when Gilly called. He didn't have to go far to get me."

Ezra smirked. "It was lunch." He looked down at his jeans and a t-shirt. "However, we didn't waste any time going home first to pack clothes."

"You could have," I said.

"Are you kidding?" He glanced at my BFF. "The way Gilly sounded, you were arrested for murder and they were throwing away the key. Clothes were the last thing on my mind."

Gilly shrugged. "I maaay have exaggerated the tiniest bit." She held her thumb and index finger a few centimeters apart.

I chuckled. "There was a clothing outlet store on the way into town. You guys should go and get checked in, then go shopping."

"Do we need to wear anything special?"

I looked him up and down, from his size eleven boots to his firm thighs to his tight waist and broad shoulders. "I think anything you wear is going to be special."

"Lederhosen it is," he quipped.

I choked back a laugh. "Does the outfit come with a side of yodeling?"

"You mean like the way Nora was yodeling last night?" Gilly asked.

My eyes widened as I pressed my hand to my chest and gave my best friend a WTF? glance.

"It was more like a night at the opera." Pippa smiled. "She leaned back against Jordy and turned her head to look at him. "If you're lucky, I might hum you a few bars later."

Jordy grinned at her. "I always feel lucky."

Ezra raised his brow at me.

"This is your fault," I told him.

"I know," he said with a knowing smirk. I swear his chest puffed up a few inches. "And the private concert was worth so much more than the price of admission."

"Okay," Gilly said. "That's enough. I mean, I know I started the whole thing, but I can only take so much loved-up-ness before I start feeling left out."

I jutted my lower lip. "Awww. Poor Gilly." I walked over to her and threw my arms around her. Pippa came in from the side, and soon we were in a BFF hug huddle. "I never want you to feel left out."

"Good, because I've been meaning to ask..." She paused.

"What? Ask away," I said.

"Anything at all," Pippa told her.

"You guys missed the announcement at the end of the PDO Threads demo, but Nurse Mary is having a Botox party in her suite tonight. Anybody who wanted to come could sign up."

"You didn't?" I blinked at her. "Seriously, Gils."

"I signed all three of us up," Gilly said.

"I'm not going to spend the weekend with a frozen face," I protested. "I like having facial expressions."

"You don't have to get it done if you don't want to, but you do have to come along."

I turned my attention to Pippa, who'd been oddly silent. "Well?"

She shrugged. "I've had it done before. It's not that big of a deal." She traced the frown line between her eyes. "I might be up for a dab here or there."

"See," Gilly said. "Even Pippa thinks it's a good idea."

Pippa snorted. "I didn't say that." Then she shook her head. "I'm just kidding. It'll be fun."

"And they are serving cocktails!" Now that she had Pippa's support, Gilly escalated the hard sale. "And Nurse Mary is cutting the price from four hundred dollars to one hundred."

"That's a good price." Pippa's enthusiasm ratcheted up another notch.

"Damn right it is." Gilly glanced at me, her eyes pleading. "So, can we go?"

"The Selebrate launch is at seven. When is this Botox party?"

"It's at nine o'clock. We have dinner with the guys at five, but the line for the Selebrate thing opens at six-thirty, when it's done, we head up to Nurse Mary's suite. Bing, bang, boom."

We broke our huddle. "You got it all figured out, huh?"

"Yep." She frowned. "There's only one thing you might not like. Carmen Carraway signed up for the party. I saw her name on the paperwork."

"Actually, that sounds perfect. I can talk to Carmen on the pretense of burying the hatchet—"

"In her back," Pippa said.

Carmen was a potential lead when it came to Samantha's "accidental" death. I worried that I was leading my friends down a rabbit hole that had an empty bottom. What if her death was nothing more than bad luck? Or in Samantha's case, bad fish. Still, I couldn't shake the feeling that someone killed that poor girl. The Botox party would be an opportunity for me to explore new leads.

"Okay," I finally said. "I'll go."

"Yay!" Gilly clapped her hands. "Now, let's get the boys settled."

Ezra and Jordy had gone to the front desk during our moment, and they walked back over, both giving us a slight head shake.

"The inn's full," Ezra said. "We'll have to try the Marlon."

Aaron approached us at that moment. He was holding

a dry-cleaning bag, two full shopping totes, and a purple orchid in a decorative pot.

"Are you just now getting back from your trip to the dry cleaners?" I asked.

"And to the Cheese Emporium, Dahlia's Deli, and a candle shop. Carmen wanted me to pick up some last-minute items for tonight."

"I thought her keynote thing wasn't until tomorrow afternoon," I said.

"She talked Belliza into footing the extra cost for Mary Graves' event tonight. And Mary has agreed to carry our skincare line exclusively."

"Wow, that's a big get," I had to admit.

"Nurse Mary and Dr. Corrine have clinics in every state," Aaron agreed. "Carmen is good at her job." He glanced around at Jordy and Ezra, his eyes widening at the two men who stuck out like sore thumbs in a room full of toes. "Who are your new friends?" he asked with some interest.

"Aaron Keller, this is Ezra Holden," I told him. "Ezra. Aaron."

Ezra smiled. "My friends call me Easy."

Aaron smiled back. "I bet they do."

Was Aaron flirting with my boyfriend? Ezra was a cutie, so it's not like I could blame him.

Pippa introduced her fella. "This is Jordy Hines. My boyfriend," she announced.

He gave her a funny look, and she gave him one back. Something was going on between those two, but what?

Jordy waved. "I'd shake your hand, but they seem a little full right now."

"Okay," Aaron said with a grin. "Maybe later." He sighed. "I better get the cheese in a fridge before it goes bad, or ages more, or whatever." He nodded to Jordy and Ezra. "Nice to meet you both." He looked at me. "Are we still on for lunch tomorrow?"

Oh, crap. I'd forgotten about lunch. I was tempted to blow Aaron off but decided against it. "Yep. And maybe we'll see you tonight at the party."

When he started to walk away, a white piece of paper floated to the floor. Ezra picked it up. He looked at it then said, "Hey, Aaron. You dropped this."

Aaron gave him a grateful glance, took the paper from Ezra, and rushed off.

"He's an odd one," Ezra said. "Seems nice enough, though."

"He was flirting with you," I told him.

Ezra smiled. "Luckily, I only have eyes for you." He kissed me right in the middle of the lobby, and I swear my toes curled.

"Lucky, lucky me." I glanced in the direction Aaron had headed. "What did he drop?"

"Dry cleaning and tailor ticket. Wine stain removal and right pocket repair," he said. "It was two hundred dollars."

"Damn, that's expensive," Gilly said.

"It's an expensive outfit." I patted Ezra's chest. "You and Jordy should go see if they have any rooms left across the road and go get some clothes."

"And we'll see if anyone will talk to us about the sushi place while we're there," Jordy added. Jordy had the kind of personality that made him the perfect barista or bartender. Even with all his tattoos and biker vibes, he exuded more calm than anyone I knew, and I'd seen with my own eyes how people lowered their guard when he was around.

"That sounds like a plan. Meet us back here at four-thirty, and we'll all grab dinner," I said. "We have a reservation at the Southwest Station Grill for dinner at five. I'll call and tell them our table of three needs to be changed to a table of five."

"That place has great enchiladas," Ezra said. He kissed me on the forehead, followed by a peck on the lips, then he and Jordy took off.

As we walked toward the elevators, Gilly asked, "Can we make that a table for six?"

"Six?"

"Luke." She smiled at me.

"He asked you out after all that?" Luke had been unsettled by my gift and what I'd revealed.

Gilly shook her head. "I asked him."

Pippa clapped her on the back. "Good for you. Way to take the initiative."

"Well, I figured I only had two more days to get his attention, so I don't have time for him to slow play a seduction."

"A seduction, huh?" I cracked a smile.

"I know when a man is interested, Nora." She pulled her shoulders back, her hips swinging with sass. "And that man is interested."

I didn't dispute her claim, because a blind man would

have noticed that Luke was attracted to Gilly. "I'll ask for an upgrade to a table for six."

"Great." Her walk became almost bouncy, and I couldn't hide my grin. I loved seeing my friend happy.

Still, something was bothering me. But I couldn't put my finger on it. It was like when you looked at a light and developed a floater in your vision, but no matter how hard you looked at it, it's just always out of view. That's how this felt.

Pippa glanced at me while we waited for the elevator. "What's wrong?"

"Nothing." I clenched my hands into fists then shook them out. "I feel like there's something I'm forgetting. I just don't know what it is."

"I'm sure it will come to you," Gilly said. "Just give it some time."

We got on the elevator. Pippa stuck her hand in her purse and fidgeted.

I pinned her with my gaze. "What's wrong with you?"

"Nothing." She sighed. "I was going to wait until after your birthday to tell you because I wanted to celebrate you this weekend, and not make it about me, but I can't keep it from you guys any longer. I'm about to burst."

"Cripes," Gilly said. "Are you sick?"

Worry gripped me. Pippa had been pukey after the eggs this morning. What if that had been a symptom of a bigger problem. "I think you better tell us."

"I'm not sick," she said. "I'm pregnant."

"Oh, my gawd!" Gilly screamed. "Holy wiener schnitzel in a gigantic baby bun. How could you not tell us?"

"That's not all," she said, her hand still in her purse. She withdrew a small black box from the bag and opened it up. Inside was a beautifully elegant princess-cut diamond. "Jordy asked me to marry him."

"And?" I said with so much anticipation, I thought I might burst.

"I said yes!"

We all squealed and hugged. After, Pippa put the ring on her left index finger. "Jordy is no longer my boyfriend. He is officially my fiancé."

"When did this happen?" I asked.

"I haven't been to the doctor yet, but I'm about three weeks late, so I took the test Wednesday night. When I came out of the bathroom with a pink plus, as bold as can be on the stick, Jordy dropped down on one knee, with ring in hand. He told me that I was the love of his life and that it would make him the proudest man in the world if I would consent to be his wife."

Gilly clutched her chest. "That's so sweet."

I wiped a tear from my cheek. "I'm so freaking happy for you."

"Yeah?" Pippa asked. "I know you have a thing about kids."

Gilly laughed, her own tears flowing now. "Nora loves kids as long as they belong to someone else. Just ask Marco and Ari."

"It's true," I said. I hugged my friend again. "And I'm going to love your baby." I glanced down at her ring again. "It really is perfect. Elegant, just like you."

And it was on her left hand. Because the left hand was

the side engagement rings were worn on. "I got it," I said. "I know what was bothering me."

Aaron had said that Carmen had torn her pocket with her engagement ring. But according to Ezra, the right pocket had been repaired. Then there was the red thread on Samantha's skirt. Coincidence? Maybe. But why would Carmen lie to her assistant about how she tore her outfit?

# CHAPTER 17

*I*t was after three when we got up to the room. We all talked and laughed and cried happy tears about Pippa and Jordy's impending nuptials and her pregnancy. She said she'd started getting morning sickness about a week earlier.

"I thought I was getting the flu," she laughed.

"A real honest-to-goodness shotgun wedding," Gilly teased.

"He said he bought the ring in July, he'd just been waiting for the perfect moment. He said the positive pregnancy test had been more perfect than he'd ever imagined."

"He's very romantic," I said. "I am so thrilled for you."

Inside, I was a swirl of chaotic emotions. On the one hand, I was extremely happy for my bestie. On the other hand, I couldn't help but worry about Ezra. He'd had his son Mason at a young age, and he'd said he didn't want any more children, but we'd never discussed marriage.

We'd only been together since March, so I hadn't thought I'd have to worry about what I would say if we reached a point where Ezra might want to make things official. However, Pippa and Jordy had started dating around the same time we had, and they were ready. The idea that Ezra might want to take that next step scared me a little. I worried it might spell the end of us, and I didn't want that. I wanted to spend every day with Ezra.

I just didn't want to have to get married to do it.

"You should have told us sooner. I would have loved to have spent a weekend celebrating your news and skipping the whole turning fifty-two thing."

Gilly sucked her teeth. "You know, not celebrating doesn't magically make the birthday not happen."

"From the woman who stopped counting birthdays at thirty-nine," I pointed out with a laugh.

"Yep, and it's a celebration every year that I don't hit forty."

Pippa beamed a smile at us. "Do you guys know how much I love you?"

"A lot," Gilly said.

"More," Pippa replied. "Think infinity."

"I love us," I told them. And we all hugged again.

After, I sat down on the edge of the bed, my mind tumbling with fears that I usually kept on lockdown. I had to focus on something else. Something that would drive me less crazy. "I'm going down to the coffee shop. You guys want anything? I can pick up snacks since we missed lunch."

"We're going to dinner soon, so don't buy any food,"

Pippa stated. "Besides, Gilly packed a suitcase full of goodies. But I will take a venti almond milk latte, half-caff, no whip, extra sugar," she answered. "I heard cravings don't start right away, but I think this baby has a sweet tooth

"Mocha Frappuccino, extra mocha, extra whip," Gilly said. "If you're buying."

"I am." I blew her a kiss. I got up from the bed. "I'll be right back."

"Maybe I should text the orders to your phone," Pippa said.

I laughed. "Your orders are complicated, so that's probably a good idea." I grabbed my purse and slid on my shoes. "I'll be right back."

Once I was out in the hall, I headed to the elevators and pushed the down button. I leaned back against the wall, closed my eyes, and took a deep breath. Change was both scary and inevitable. It's a concept I tended to embrace. However, I needed a few minutes to myself to wrap my head around all the wonderful news Pippa had unpacked.

The soft shuffle of feet on the carpet forced me to open my eyes. I stiffened as Gregory walked toward me. "Are you following me?"

"My executive suite is on this floor in the northeast corner, Nora. I'm not stalking you if that's what you're worried about." Gregory was much calmer than he'd been the night before, but his voice lacked warmth. I couldn't forget the way he'd grabbed me, and I was leery of letting down my guard. I'd been battered enough this year. I didn't plan to keep making it a habit. So, I hugged my purse to my body, ready to bolt or defend myself, and hoping like hell I wouldn't have to do either.

When I didn't say any more to him, Gregory said, "I'm sorry about last night. I was obviously distressed. Samantha hadn't been my assistant long. Even so, her death was a shock."

I nodded. "I can imagine." Only, he'd seemed a lot more worried about his launch party and whatever item he'd thought was missing. I suspected it was Samantha's tablet, but I didn't know for sure. I took a chance that he wouldn't go postal and asked, "Did you find what you were looking for?"

His shoulders raised, and his body tensed at the question. "I have not. I'm sure it will turn up somewhere."

"Are you still demonstrating your meditation pod at the launch party?"

"Yes. There's no point in having a launch if we're not going to show the beauty industry why our machine is better than..."

"Then Konash Technology's Zensation?"

Gregory eyed me with suspicion. "Our pod is better. We have the latest in binaural waves to realign your mind. Plus, our aromatherapy cool-steam system can be changed at a tap of the button to increase energy, help you relax, or even boost creativity. And the comfort in our tech is unrivaled."

"Okay, but you also only have one working meditation pod." Before he could deny it, I held my hand up. "I heard you talking to Samantha yesterday, remember?"

"Right. When you were eavesdropping," he said tartly.

"If you want privacy, don't argue in a public hallway."

"We weren't arguing."

The elevator doors opened, and we both went into the car. I pushed the button for the first floor. "Are you going to disclose Samantha's death to the volunteers before they get inside?"

Gregory hit number six. "The Stress-less didn't kill her. Besides, we cleaned the damn thing from top to bottom and replaced the gel memory foam pads."

"Of course, you did. You wouldn't want people to think you give a damn about your assistant taking her last breath in there."

Gregory furrowed his brows and glared at me. "I resent your implications. If you must know, Carmen will demonstrate the pod. No one else will be allowed in it."

She must really love him, I thought, to crawl into the death machine. "Did you find out if the pod had been sabotaged? Is it dangerous for Carmen to use it?"

"You really are a busybody, Nora. Why do you even care?" The elevators opened on the sixth floor. "But no," Gregory said as he exited then turned back to look at me. "The pod was never sabotaged. It is in perfect working order, and today's demo will make its superiority clear."

I had been going to the coffee shop on the first floor, but I stopped the doors before they could close and stepped out. Impulsively, I reached out and touched Gregory's sleeve. When the lines around his eyes softened, I withdrew my hand.

"Why is this so important, Gregory?"

He stiffened again. "I don't know what you mean."

"Come on. You're jumping through hoops to make this launch happen, no matter the consequences. I know it's been a while, but I don't remember you as being this coldhearted."

His brown eyes hardened. "I wish you would leave this alone. I'm...I'm counting on this launch. I need the Stress-less to impress industry buyers."

"Any buyers in particular?" Aaron had said he'd bought stuff for the Botox party for Carmen. He also implied that she had managed to wrangle a contract to sell Belliza products exclusively at the surgical and aesthetic chain.

Sanduski and Nurse Mary had one to two clinics in almost every state. Was Carmen angling to get the billion-dollar chain in the meditation pod business as well? That would put pods in each shop, at over thirty thousand dollars a unit, which meant a three million dollar plus deal. It was a lot of money in the real world, but in corporate world terms, it was a good get, but not a make-or-break kind of thing.

"You're working a deal with Nurse Mary and Dr. Sanduski to furnish pods for their clinics, aren't you?"

"How do you know?" He looked spooked.

I didn't need a supernatural sniffer to make these deductions. The trail was there for anyone to see if they were looking. "And if they buy from you, it will give you an inside to other beauty clinics across America."

"The world," Gregory agreed tightly. He stepped up to me. I moved to the side so that he wasn't smack in front of me. "Langford can't find out. He'll try to undercut me," he hissed.

"I don't even know the guy," I said. "I'm not trying to mess with your business." But Langford had been in Samantha's hotel room. Had she been sharing company secrets with him? Or had she been playing the Konash executive on Gregory's behalf? There were at least a dozen people, hotel staff and such, milling around the floor. If Gregory was tempted to get nasty with me again, he wouldn't do it in front of an audience. "Was Samantha spying on Brian Langford for you?"

His jaw dropped, then as if on a hinge, he stuttered, "I...I...I..."

It was true. Gregory had encouraged his assistant to spy for him. "You put that girl's life in jeopardy, and for what? Money?"

"She died from eating ill-prepared fugu," he said by way of denial. "Her death had nothing to do with business."

"Keep telling yourself that," I was angry and disappointed. "Samantha wasn't a prostitute to be pimped out so that you could land a deal. It's disgusting, Gregory."

"It was her idea." His gaze grew distant. "She said she had something to show me. We were supposed to meet in her hotel room, but she never returned. Then the hotel manager contacted me..."

"Because we'd found her."

He nodded. "I don't know why she would have gone to the display." He balled his fist and smacked it against his outer thigh. "The R and D on this meditation pod has cost the company more money than we can afford. If the deal with Sanduski doesn't go through, we might not recover. Especially if Konash gets the Zensation out there before us. I think Samantha had found proof that Langford was guilty of industrial espionage."

"Is that why you searched her room after security had sealed the door?"

"How did you..." He took a big step back to put distance between us. "I'm done with this conversation, Nora."

Even so, he'd confirmed what I'd suspected. "If you tell me the truth, I might be able to help you."

He scoffed. "You're not a detective. You're not even in the beauty industry anymore. You're a small-town crafter. You make soap, for God's sake. If you really want to help, mind your own damn business."

I watched Gregory stroll away. At the end of the hall, he stopped to talk to the security guard Raul. They could have been finalizing security plans for the launch, but the way Raul turned a withering stare at me, made my stomach clench. The large man started walking my way. I reached back and tapped the down button on the elevator, praying the doors would open.

They did. I quickly stepped inside, never taking my eyes off the intimidating man, and pushed the button for the lobby. Then, I held down the *door closed* button as Raul got within twenty feet of the elevator.

The security guard crossed his arms and watched me as the metal doors slid shut between us.

Only then did I let out the breath I'd been holding. I was pretty sure now how Gregory had managed to search a sealed room and replace the tape. I wondered how much it had cost him to buy Raul? Less than what he'd lose if the Stress-less wasn't a success. If Raul would take money to help him illegally search a dead woman's room, what else would he do for money? Would he kill? Maybe.

But unlikely. Especially with everyone convinced Samantha had died accidentally.

And that's what bothered me the most. Gregory, the hotel staff, hell, even the police were so eager to believe Samantha's death was a deadly case of food poisoning. No one wanted to explore the other option.

Samantha had been murdered.

# CHAPTER 18

*A*t five o'clock, Luke was waiting for us outside the Southwest Station Grill. He'd changed into more casual wear, dark blue denim jeans and a polo shirt. Gilly, who took the longest of the three of us to get ready, was dressed in a black wraparound dress that, with the added lift of a push-up bra, put all kinds of va-va into her voom.

Southwest Station Grill had not only allowed me to change the reservation, they'd also been enthusiastic when I asked them for a little help with a surprise. The decor was southwest with lots of pale greens, blues, and taupe. They had coyotes and other southwest-themed accents carved into copper lampshades that hung over every table. There was a large bar at the center of the place, and there wasn't a single empty barstool. The main floor was packed with diners, nearly every booth and table full. I'd been fortunate that they agreed to make our increased party size work.

The waitstaff had put two tables together to accommodate the six of us, and I couldn't help but smile when Luke pulled Gilly's chair out for her.

"You're beautiful," he told her as she sat down.

"I clean up okay," Gilly replied modestly.

"I don't just mean now," he said. "I mean, all the time."

Dang. I had actual butterflies for my BFF. And speaking of butterflies. Ezra and Jordy, not to be outdone by the newcomer, held out our chairs as well.

I giggled. I didn't need anyone to pull out my chair or open doors for me, but it was a sweet gesture. Pippa unrolled her napkin, her ring on display.

Ezra nudged me. "She finally told you, huh?"

"You knew?"

"Jordy told me on the drive up," he admitted. "He asked me to be his best man."

"What's going on?" Luke asked.

"Pippa and Jordy got engaged," Gilly blurted. "And they're having a baby!"

Ezra looked at me. "He didn't tell me that." He got up from his chair and went around the table to bro-hug Jordy. "Congrats, man. A baby. That's great. You're going to be a great dad."

"And a wonderful husband," I added.

Jordy's smile was so wide it split his face. "I can't wait," he said. "For both." He leaned over and kissed Pippa. "I'm glad you told them because I want the world to know. I'm the luckiest man on Earth."

Ezra came back to our side of the table and sat down again. He leaned over and whispered, "Jordy has some competition for the luckiest man."

I grinned. "I'm the lucky one."

Luke said to Gilly, "This seems more like a close friends' kind of celebration. Are you sure you want me here?"

"The more the merrier," Jordy said.

"Besides," Gilly said, as she hit him with her most charming smile. "Without you, I'd be the only gal without a plus one."

"All right, then." Luke picked up the menu. "The enchiladas are good here."

Ezra stretched his hand across the table for a high-five. "My man," he said.

Luke obliged him with a soft high-five in front of my face. I grinned at Gilly. We both laughed. *Men*.

The aroma of chili, garlic, lime, and grilled onions popped me in and out of a few childhood memories. Gilly eating tacos with me from the Taco Shake Shack, Ezra sitting at a table with his son Mason, also eating tacos. Garden Cove was limited on the Mexican food front, but I would put the Taco Shake Shack's tacos up against anyone's.

I struggled to see the menu items until Gilly handed me her reading glasses without comment.

"Oh, they have tacos al pastor," I said as I scanned the menu. "I'm getting an order of those and an avocado salad." I'd been doing some stomach crunches lately, but I felt like there was no flattening my post-hysterectomy belly. Even so... "Or maybe I'll skip the tacos."

"Oh, hell no," Gilly said. "We're celebrating. You are having tacos."

The waiter, a guy named Guillermo, came over and took our drink orders.

I turned my attention to Luke. "Have you heard anything else about Samantha? Did you find anything in her room?"

"Other than the gun, nothing suspicious. It was a little messy, but some guests are messy."

"So, no pink tablet?"

"Nope. Her purse was in here, with her wallet, but no phone, either."

"That's strange," I said.

"Tell him about Paramount," Ezra said.

I had told them all about my encounter with Gregory. Pippa and Gilly, when I'd brought the drinks back up to the room, then I'd retold the story when we met up with Ezra and Jordy. This would be my third time.

"What's this about?" Luke asked.

I looked at Luke. "I'm fairly certain Gregory is the person who went into Samantha's room to search it."

"How?" he asked. "I mean, even if he had an extra keycard to his assistant's room, he didn't have access to the security tape."

"No, but Raul did."

"Raul?" Luke blinked at me as if I'd grown an extra head. "Did you have one of your smelly thingies?"

He made my gift sound like farting. "No. Just deductive reasoning. Gregory told me that he'd basically pimped his assistant out to spy on the competition to see if they were behind the sabotage of the Stress-less pod."

"And where does Raul fit in?"

"After I confronted him about searching her room, he hightailed it down the hall to speak with Raul. They were both staring me down. Then Raul started heading in my direction."

"The tape isn't easily accessible," mused Luke. "But Raul—like everyone else on the security team—knows where it's located." He met my gaze. "Raul's been working for three months. He's an ex-marine. He takes care of his sick father, and he's proven himself capable in a lot of situations. You really think Raul and Paramount are working together?"

"Money makes some people do things they wouldn't normally." Raul caring for his father made me think of my mom. It had been hard being the one, but I wouldn't have missed a minute of having her alive and with me for the time we had left. "Look, it's just a feeling. Maybe I read the situation wrong."

Luke's lips thinned. "Even so, I'll look into it."

The waiter came back with four ice teas, a Diet Coke for Gilly, and a bottle of sparkling water for Pippa. Guillermo took our food orders and went back to the kitchen.

After he was gone, Ezra focused back on the investigation. "The sushi place at the Marlon has been closed. The front desk clerk told me that the cook and staff wouldn't be back for a few days." He shook his head. "I didn't try to embarrass her about it. I mean, what was she supposed to say. I'm sure the restaurant will be out of business until the health department does a thorough check, and the place will have to get rid of whatever fugu they have on hand."

"That's an expensive mistake," Luke said. "But if it caused Ms. Jones' death, then they should be shut down."

I was glad to see he wasn't the kind of guy who got his feathers ruffled easily. Some men, especially cops, or ex-cops in Luke's case, could be territorial. But Luke didn't act like he minded. Maybe, because of it being the anniversary of his friend's death, he welcomed the distraction. Even if it didn't amount to a hill of beans.

Ezra leaned back in his chair. "I called a doctor friend of mine back home. He works as our medical examiner in Garden Cove. I asked about tetrodotoxin since I've never had a case involving the poison. The only thing I'd ever really heard about it is that it makes zombies."

I snickered. "There's no such thing as zombies." We'd spent a weekend in July doing a *Walking Dead* marathon with his son Mason, while we'd all debated the viability of zombies.

"Tell that to Rick Grimes," he bantered. "Apparently, though, it's tough to test for tetrodotoxin because the amount that makes it into blood and urine is so scant that it sometimes doesn't show up. The only other way is to test her stomach contents to see if there is any of the fugu fish in there, but that takes a few days. It turns out that poisoning is usually determined by exposure plus symptoms."

Jordy spoke up, "The old, if it walks like a duck, and talks like a duck method."

"That's it on the nose," Ezra agreed. "That's why they were able to call it an accident so quickly. She'd eaten sushi for lunch, and she died because of respiratory failure related to paralysis. All consistent with tetrodotoxin poisoning."

"So, it paralyzed her lungs, and she suffocated," I said. It definitely explained the blue tinge to her skin.

Ezra nodded. "Yep."

"That's terrible," Pippa said. She teared up, then aggressively wiped at her eyes with her napkin. "I'm sorry. I don't know why I can't seem to keep my emotions under control."

"It's called hormonal imbalance." Gilly, who was next to Pippa, gave her a comforting pat on the hand. "Welcome to the wonderful roller coaster ride known as your first trimester."

"The last two weeks, I've cried and slept more than I have in the past two years. It gets better, right?"

Gilly laughed. "Oh, honey, this is just the warm-up." She gave Pippa another pat. "I loved being pregnant. Just wait until you feel Jordy Junior or Pippa the Second having a dance party in your belly. It's magical." Then she turned to Luke. "I have two kids—seventeen-year-old twins—who are starting their senior year next week. I've been divorced for a decade. Also, I'm a Capricorn, you know, just in case you're into that astrology stuff." She smiled at him. "Your turn."

He flushed then looked around the table as we all waited expectantly. "Well...you already know I was a military investigator. I was in for twenty-two years before I retired last year. Did three years of college for a criminal justice degree right out of high school. I dropped out to join the Army and went to basic training. Decided I didn't love being a grunt, finished my degree online, went to officer training school, and the rest is history." He smiled at her. "Oh, and I'm a Taurus."

"Never married?" I asked, unable to help myself.

"Engaged once," he admitted. "But I spent my military career all over the states and in Europe. It's hard to settle down when your job has wings."

"So, no kids?" Pippa asked.

Gilly didn't even try to stop us from prying. Pippa was so unapologetically fierce, she just looked at Luke and waited for his answer.

"Not that I'm aware of." He choked out a laugh. "I've been through interrogation training that was less intense." He met Gilly's gaze. "So, am I guilty?"

"Only if being cute is a crime."

Pippa sipped her sparkling water, the diamond in her ring glinted as it caught the light. Dang it. I'd got so caught up with all the news and the encounter with Gregory, that I forgot about the red thread on the skirt and in Carmen's jumper. "Did anyone note the small red thread on Samantha's pink skirt? I thought it was probably contact lint. I mean, I get stuff sticking to my clothes all the time, but maybe it means more."

"The coroner didn't mention anything about a loose red thread in evidence. Why do you think it might be important?" Luke asked.

"Carmen had a rip in the pocket of the outfit she wore yesterday. She had her assistant get it cleaned and tailored today instead of waiting until she got home. That in itself isn't overly suspicious, but tie in that she told her assistant that she'd snagged the pocket with her engagement ring. It makes me wonder what she's hiding?"

Jordy frowned. "Why is that suspicious?"

I glanced over at Ezra. His eyes lit up. "Because the

repair was to the right pocket. And women wear their engagement rings on their left."

"Exactly," I said.

"None of this is evidence of a crime. I mean, it sounds like there is a bunch of shady stuff going on at the convention, but none of it points to Samantha's death being anything other than what it appears to be. An accident," Luke said.

"There is that," I agreed. Everything I'd learned reminded me of the middle pieces of a jumbled puzzle, and I knew that if I could just find the corners, I could start to make sense of it all.

Our food arrived in record time, and we all dug in. And let me tell you, tacos al pastor had definitely been the right call. When everyone nearly finished, I saw five waiters—three men, including Guillermo, and two women —heading our way with two large scoops of Mexican fried ice cream topped with sparklers, and another plate of freshly fried sopapillas, also alight with sparklers. One of the guys had a bottle of sparkling cider, which I'd ordered for the sober lovebirds, and the last had a stack of plates and six champagne flutes.

I grinned at Pippa. She was smiling back.

We were both shocked when they started dancing and clapping to a Mariachi-inspired Happy Birthday, followed by a Happy Engagement. Even though my birthday wasn't until tomorrow, I was simultaneously embarrassed and delighted.

When we finished off the desserts, we had to get going. The Stress-less party was starting soon, and there was no way I was missing the potentially disastrous demonstration.

# CHAPTER 19

"It's about time," Gilly said when people finally started moving toward our ultimate destination: the Tulip Ballroom. We'd arrived at ten after six in hopes of getting a prime spot. Hah. The line already trailed down the sixth-floor hallway on both sides. Jordy and Ezra were on a sofa out in the common area, waiting for us. They wouldn't be allowed in without a convention pass, but they had wanted to be close just in case.

Luke, as head of security, had already planned to work the event, especially after Samantha's death. He stood near the door with Raul and another security guy I hadn't seen before. He'd changed out of his jeans and into his blue jacket and black suit pants again. Or a version of them.

I nodded in his direction. "Is he a quick-change artist?" I asked Gilly.

"He keeps a spare here just in case he needs them. He said he learned his lesson after tackling someone to the ground in the parking lot when he first started here. He'd ripped a huge hole in his pants and tore the jacket at the shoulder seam in the scuffle."

"Oh, yeah." Pippa made kissy faces at Gilly. "What else did he tell you?"

Gilly had volunteered to ride back to the hotel with Luke, so they'd had about ten minutes of alone time. And, while they'd left the restaurant at the same time as the rest of us, they'd come inside about five minutes later. And when they'd arrived inside, they both looked stupidly happy.

I piled on with Pippa. "Yeah, what else? I know you're keeping something from us."

Our friend blushed then turned to face Pippa and me. "He kissed me after we parked. Like several minutes of kissing." She fanned herself. "My whole body is warm just thinking about him."

"Or you're having a hot flash," I teased.

"Guuurl, if this is how a hot flash feels, then day-am, give me more."

I frowned. "If you're enjoying it, it's not a hot flash." We all laughed. I was the only one in menopause, thanks to my surgeon cutting out all my reproductive parts, but the hormone replacement therapy helped keep the hot flashes mostly at bay. Whew, though. When they happened, it was flop-sweat central on my body.

"He's a good kisser, huh?" I asked grinning.

"That man has mastered kissing," she replied a bit dreamily. She craned her head past the milling line in front of us as we moved slowly toward the entrance to catch Luke's eye. She waved. He gave her a sappy smile and waved back. "I can still feel him on my lips."

"I think the feeling is mutual," Pippa said. "He couldn't take his eyes off you at dinner."

"Still can't," I said when I noticed how often he scanned the swarm of guests for Gilly.

"If only he didn't live so far away," she sighed.

"It's only two hours. Quicker if you drive like Ezra."

Pippa giggled. "Jordy told me Ezra used his cop light on the highway. He said he's been in slower street races."

So, that's what Ezra had meant when he'd said he'd broken a few laws. I sighed happily. Gilly and Pippa did the same. "I know this was supposed to be a girls' weekend for my birthday, but I think this is somehow better." I grimaced. "Minus the dead body, of course."

"Of course," my friends both agreed as we sobered a little.

I glanced at Ezra on the couch, and we locked gazes. He winked at me, and my heart skipped a beat. "I'm so happy, you guys. I'm happy for me, and I'm happy for both of you. And the thing I've learned by being at this conference is, I don't miss any bit of my old life—none of it. I haven't once been like, oh, I wish that was me. No. I'm just thrilled to be here with the two of you, but I think next year we can just come to the city for fun."

"We've both known you a long time, Nora. So, we were already aware you were happier than you'd been in forever," Pippa said. "But I'm glad you finally see it."

"Aww." Gilly put her arm around me. "You're Dorothy from *The Wizard of Oz*, finally figuring out that there's no place like home."

"You guys are a laugh riot," I said as we progressed forward.

Raul was checking ID badges, and he curled his lip at me when I showed him mine. Eep. I was glad Luke was standing right behind him. The ballroom was divided into two sections, and a white curtain enclosed a raised platform at the front of the room. The event coordinators had put seating in a half circle around the curtained-off area with rows of chairs, stadium-style. Two aisles created three sections.

"Let's see how close we can get," I said. I would have preferred front and center, but the middle section had filled up fast. We ended up in the third row on the left-hand side.

"This isn't too bad," Pippa said.

Apparently, the aromatherapy machine was going full blast. "I smell lemon verbena again."

"Fun fact," Gilly said. "Lemon verbena is good for relieving stress and anxiety. I use it sometimes on particularly tense clients."

Pippa smoothed her hands down her thighs to her knees. "I might need a whole vat of the stuff after this weekend is over."

"Samesies," Gilly and I said at the same time.

"Jinx," Gilly called first. "You owe me a Diet Coke."

At seven o'clock, Gregory stepped up onto the platform. He had a microphone attached to his collar, so his voice was amplified.

"Welcome, welcome," he said to the crowd as they applauded his entrance. "I'm Gregory Paramount, CEO of Selebrate, and I'm thrilled to welcome you to the preeminent launch of the most cutting-edge meditation pod to ever hit the market."

He made a little fist pump out in front of him, and everyone clapped again.

"Are you ready?" he asked the enthusiastic crowd. The lights went down in the room, and the stage lit up. A spotlight followed Gregory as he stepped down to the floor in front of the platform.

I looked at Gilly and Pippa, and they both rolled their eyes.

"The crowd seems hyped," Pippa said. "I've seen half a dozen big spa reps in the audience. If the demo goes well, it means big bucks for Selebrate."

"That's what he's banking on." There was some movement on our side of the curtain. Pink hair poked out from behind, followed by Blanche's smiling face. She waved at me.

My eyes wide, I waved back. "What is Blanche doing?"

Gilly shrugged. "Maybe she's helping with the demonstration."

"Gregory had said Carmen was going to be in the pod."

"Maybe Blanche is assisting," Pippa ventured.

I nodded. "That's probably it." Though, why hadn't she told me she was working the launch when we'd talked about it this morning?

Music began to play.

"Oh my gosh," Gilly whispered. "That's the theme song from *2001: A Space Odyssey*."

The music began to build as he declared, "And now if

you're ready, I present to you the Stress-less Meditation Pod!"

I couldn't help but smile as an enthusiastic Blanche pushed the curtain around to expose the display. More cheering ensued, but my pals and I had already seen the science fiction setup. It looked much as it had in the Rosewood Room, except for a large-screen monitor that had been added to the mix. It was rotated so that it faced the spectators.

The volume of the music lowered. There was a man I didn't recognize in a lab jacket on the stage. He stood next to the pod, pointing out all the vital elements as Gregory described the special features.

"Cool gel technology that puts your body at the exact right temperature for maximum pain and stress relief," Gregory said. "That, combined with space-age memory foam, gives the user a sense of weightlessness. The dome —or the egg, as my fiancée calls it—lifts when you wave your hand under the sensor."

Lab Coat Guy waved his hand under the front, and the lid opened, its lights swirling, a light fog behind it, giving it a grand feeling.

"Inside the dome is an exclusive aromatherapy aerosolizer that creates the perfect forty-five percent humidity inside the pod for the most relaxed breathing. It can be adjusted higher to relieve chest congestion in folks with breathing disorders.

Lab Coat Guy spun the front of the pod toward the audience and indicated the interior of the door. It just looked like a bunch of dots to me. Still, folks clapped.

"We have the most advanced noise-canceling padding,

and the pod has blackout capability, so you feel like you are floating in space." The lights dramatically went out, and when they came back up, Blanche was inside the pod. "Just thirty minutes in the Stress-less pod will make you feel as if you've spent an entire day at the spa."

"Wait," Pippa said. "I thought Carmen was the guinea pig for this demonstration."

I hadn't seen Carmen since we'd arrived, but I'd assumed she'd make her entrance much in the same fashion as Gregory. What in the world was Blanche doing?"

I glared at Gregory. His gaze flicked to mine before he quickly looked away. Why lie to me about who would be demonstrating the pod? It didn't make any sense.

He stepped back up on the stage and leaned in close to Blanche. "Are you ready for an experience that will revolutionize the way you think about de-stressing?"

"Uhm, sure," Blanche said brightly. "Let's do it."

She winked at me. What the hell was that woman up to?

Lab Coat Guy waved his hand at the front of the dome again, and it lowered over Blanche. My stomach did a double flip as I remembered Samantha's legs sticking out. It would be fine, I told myself. Gregory wouldn't be doing this if he thought his machine was unsafe, right? He wasn't stupid, but his money problems might make him reckless. Still, everything seemed to be working right so far.

I worried my hands until Pippa and Gilly each grabbed one.

The monitor turned on, and Blanche's face, in

grayscale, showed up. There had to be a camera inside the pod. Blanche's eyes and teeth glowed under the night-vision setting.

Gregory pushed a button on the pod that triggered a speaker inside the shell. "Are you comfortable?" he asked her.

"This is great," Blanche said.

"Then, it's time to begin." He nodded to Lab Coat Guy, who pushed a few more buttons. The machine purred alive. We all watched with bated breath as Blanche closed her eyes. Everything seemed to be going okay. So far so good.

"Stop!" a woman yelled from the back.

Everyone turned. Remy Tarlington took off a long brunette wig as she moved from middle-row seating and into the aisle. There was a collective gasp at the reveal.

With major dramatic flair, she threw the wig onto the floor and jabbed an accusing finger toward Gregory. "This man is a liar," she shouted. "A liar and a thief. He stole my design. Stress-less is my work. Mine!"

Another round of gasps occurred when she pulled a gun out and started waving it around.

Without having to talk about it, Pippa, Gilly, and I got onto the floor.

Raul tackled her from behind, and we all watched, horrified, as Luke retrieved her gun and put cuffs on her. After, they dragged her from the ballroom.

"Cripes," Gilly said breathlessly. "That was terrifying."

"Agreed." My heart drummed as I turned my attention back to the pod and the monitor. "Oh no." Amid Remy's meltdown, no one had been paying attention to Blanche.

"She's clawing at her throat," I hissed as I jumped to my feet. "Get her out of there!" I yelled.

Gregory paled as he turned to look at the video screen. He waved his hand under the dome, but it didn't raise. "Get it open," he ordered Lab Coat Guy. "Get it open now!"

# CHAPTER 20

*L*ab Coat Guy's name was Jackson Miller, and he was an engineer in the development department at Selebrate. He was now considering a new career in a field that was less stressful, like bomb disposal.

I knew all this because he'd had a panic attack after it took three tries of the emergency dome release to get Blanche out of the pod. I'd spent a few minutes helping to calm him down while he breathed into a paper bag. There had been a plastic surgeon in the audience, and he'd tended to Blanche until the paramedics arrived.

Ezra had his arm around me as the medics worked on Blanche. After Pippa complained of feeling woozy, Gilly took her to the common area to sit with Jordy.

Blanche complained of shortness of breath, and she'd rasped out that her throat felt thick, and she couldn't swallow her own spit. The medics had treated her for an allergic reaction by giving her a dose of epinephrine and Benadryl. It hadn't helped, but at least she was still breathing. They'd taken her to the common area, just in case whatever she'd reacted to was still in the vicinity. After, they put her on four liters of oxygen because her blood oxygen saturation had dropped down to eighty-seven percent. I knew from taking care of my mom that normal was ninety-five percent or better.

"Nora," Blanche wheezed as they raised the gurney for transport. She floated her fingers toward me. "Nora."

I walked over and took her hand. "You'll be okay," I told her. "You're in good hands."

"Tried...to...help," she said. Her voice was weak and muffled under the oxygen mask.

"Help?"

"Heh-help you." She gave a weak cough and touched the oxygen tubing in her nose. At least, she was still breathing. "Invest...igate."

"Silly girl," I told her. She'd thought she was helping me and my investigation by volunteering. Instead, she'd turned herself into another part of the mystery.

"We've got to go," a female paramedic said. She twirled her finger in the air in a "wrap it up" motion.

"Take care of yourself, Blanche."

"Nora," she whispered, then followed my name with an unintelligible mumbling.

"What? I couldn't understand you."

She dragged the mask down to her chin.

I moved in closer so I could hear her.

"Soaps...like candy...candy bars."

"Huh?"

"Make...soap."

"You want me to make soaps that look like candy bars?" I asked with mild incredulity.

She smiled and nodded as the paramedic snapped her mask back into place and wheeled her toward the elevator.

"What was that all about?" Ezra asked.

"She's a fan," I said with a head shake. I saw Brian Langford watching from the hallway, a satisfied smirk on his face. "Someone ought to talk to that guy, too."

"Who?" Ezra asked.

"Langford." I pointed to the man and made sure he saw me. My glare wiped the smirk from his face. "He has as much to gain from the Stress-less failing as Gregory has to lose."

Luke had returned from taking Remy into custody, and he blew past us in the common area, headed straight toward Gregory, who was talking to Raul.

Ezra and I followed.

"Remy Tarlington sabotaged the meditation pod," Gregory accused as soon as we arrived. He glared at Luke. "When are the police coming? I want to press charges against that crazy bitch."

"They're on their way," Luke said, his voice edged with anger. "I thought you said the pod was working properly."

"It was, but Remy must have gotten into the room and messed with the pod."

Luke shook his head. "I've had security on this door nonstop since yesterday. No one unauthorized has been in or out of the room."

"Are you blaming me for what happened to the volunteer? If she was allergic to essential oils, she should have said so before agreeing to sit for the demonstration."

Speaking of volunteering, I couldn't help but interject.

"I thought Carmen was going to demonstrate the Stress-less."

Gregory gave me a scathing stare. "This is none of your business, Nora."

"But it is mine," Luke said. "So, how did Ms. Michaels end up in there instead of Ms. Carraway?"

"If you must know, she got called away for some emergency related to her party tonight." His shoulders slumped. "I won't recover from this," he said to no one in particular. "I'm going to lose everything."

"At least you'll still have your life," Luke said. He scowled at Raul. "Wait here with Mr. Paramount until the police arrive." He fixed his underling with a hard stare. "No second chances, you understand?"

Raul nodded. He gave me a quick glance then looked away. I guessed from his chagrinned expression that Luke had a "come to Jesus" talk with the man, but it didn't appear that he was going to fire him.

As we headed back into the common area, Ezra asked, "What do you think?"

"I think something stinks," I said. "But I'm not sure what. I mean, it's not like Blanche ate fugu." My chest tightened with worry. "I hope Blanche is okay."

"She was still breathing when she left." Ezra gave me a reassuring smile. "That's a good sign."

"She shouldn't have been in that damn death trap in the first place." I shook my head. "It's my fault."

"Now, don't say that."

"I told her that I was looking into Samantha's death. I'd even bragged about helping the police once or twice with an investigation. It's just that, well, she was just such a big fan, and it made me want to impress her even more." I clucked my tongue. "She volunteered tonight, thinking it would somehow help me investigate Samantha's death."

"You didn't ask her to do it, Nora. You can't control anyone's actions but your own." He kissed my temple.

"I know." I sighed. "You're right."

I spotted Jackson sitting by himself on a bench near the elevators. "Come on. I want to talk to the engineer."

We made our way over, and I sat down on the bench next to the young man. "How are you feeling?"

He nodded. "Better. Thanks for earlier."

"No worries. Panic attacks happen." I smiled sympathetically. "Hey, is there anything in that machine that could have made Blanche, the woman in the pod, have a reaction? Anything that would make her throat close or her lungs to fill constricted?"

He shook his head, then scrubbed his face. "The Stress-less is designed to enhance breathing, not make it worse. And, frankly, I had that thing running perfectly this morning. Someone had cut a few wires that controlled the temperature of the pod and the humidity level. The humidity level was still a little high, but not dangerous. And the temperature control was an easy fix. If it was an attempt to sabotage the machine, it was a poor one."

"Do you know Remy Tarlington?"

He bit his lower lip then said, "She's the one who hired me to the team." He met my gaze. "She would've known how to do the most damage if she had been the one behind the cut wires. Whatever Mr. Paramount thinks, I don't believe it was Remy. She's not that incompetent."

I could've argued that his previous boss was a bit nuts, the way she'd pulled a gun in a crowd, but I let it go. Mostly because I didn't disagree with him. There were probably a dozen ways that an engineer could've put that contraption out of order, but whoever had clipped the wires picked the easiest to fix.

"The humidity levels were high. Does that mean the aerosolizer was producing more vapor?"

"Yeah," he said, "but the FDA has deemed the aromatherapy line as safe, even at the machine's highest levels."

"Hmmm." Maybe Blanche had been allergic to one of the fragrances. "How do you load the machine with the aromatherapy?"

"There is a fill port at the back of the dome. It has slots for all six aromatherapies in the Stress-less line."

"Did you fill it yourself?"

"I didn't have to," he said. "They were all full already."

I nodded. "Thanks, Jackson." I stood up. "Good luck with the new career in bomb disposal." The kid smiled.

As we walked toward Jordy, Pippa, and Gilly, Ezra said, "He doesn't believe that woman, the one with the gun, is responsible."

"I agree with him. Remy Tarlington is angry, scared, and a little off her rocker. Still, I don't believe she's behind what happened to the pod, or what happened to Samantha and Blanche."

# CHAPTER 21

*B*y the time the police arrived, took everyone's names, cleared the scene, and dismissed us, it was time to head up to Nurse Mary's twentieth-floor penthouse suite.

I was antsy to speak with Carmen, and that was something I never thought I'd say. I wanted to gauge her reaction to what went down at the Selebrate launch. I wondered if she would stand by her man or bail on a sinking ship. It all depended on how much she loved him, I supposed, or how much she was involved in the whole rotten affair.

The guys, who had no interest in the party, stayed downstairs to hang out in the bar and watch some baseball and try to get updates on Blanche. We all agreed to meet up after the party ended.

Gilly, who hadn't lost any excitement to try Botox, practically skipped down the hall, but Pippa had me worried.

"Are you feeling well? Maybe you should go lie down,"

I suggested as we navigated the short hall that only had four doors for the four large suites that took up the entire floor.

"I think the guacamole might be working its way backward." She pressed her stomach. "I'll be fine, though. Maybe they'll have a ginger ale or something in there."

"Here it is," Gilly said. "Twenty-o-three." She perched her gaze on Pippa. "It's not too late. We can just go meet the guys and rest. We've all earned a break."

"Nope. We're doing this for you." Pippa poked a finger between Gilly's eyes. "After all, it's only a hundred dollars for a full treatment," she teased.

Gilly chortled. In her most offended tone, she asked, "Are you inferring that I might need Botox?"

"I would never infer such a thing. I'm more a say-it-straight kind of gal." Then Pippa laughed before putting her fingers to her lips and taking a deep breath. "I'm okay." She looked at Gilly. "And I'm just kidding, by the way. You barely have any frown lines. Mine are like napkin holders."

We all had our purses, plus Gilly had brought a tote just in case there were goodies. I wasn't sure what kind of take-home stuff they would have. Maybe some eye creams. The past two days, I'd developed puffy eyes. Ice and concealer only went so far.

"Do we knock?" I asked.

"I was waiting for someone to change their mind," Gilly said, not waiting for us to respond as she rapped on the door with her knuckles.

The door opened, and Aaron stood in front of us wearing another Italian suit, this one in a charcoal gray with subtle black pinstriping. "Well, hello, ladies! And Pippa," he said with a smirk. Pippa gave him a light punch to his gut, and he feigned pain as if it were a mighty blow. "Come on in. The party is just getting started." He acted tipsy.

"I'd say the party's already in full swing."

"I'm celebrating."

I laughed. The kid was funny.

He put his finger to his lips and blew a shhhhh. "Don't tell anyone."

The sharp scent of gin, along with lime, wafted in my direction.

*"If things go my way, we'll both get what we want," a man says. He is sitting in a dark corner of the hotel bar. "How does it feel to know you are going to be the youngest person to make junior executive?"*

*Another man sits down. He is holding a drink that smells of gin and lime. There is a cherry on top. A Tom Collins probably. He takes his hat off, a billed cap, and sets it on the small table. "It feels like winning." I recognize his voice as Aaron's.*

*He raises his glass then takes a sip. He pulls a maraschino cherry off the top of the ice and eats it. He is uncharacteristically dressed in jeans and a fitted t-shirt.*

*I wish I could see the faces. I think I know who the other man is, but I'm not certain.*

*"Business is business," he says. "You can't let personal feelings get in the way of ambition." He sets down a highball glass. "We'll talk more this weekend. But remember, this has to stay between us, until the official announcement. And if anyone catches wind of what you're doing, the deal is off."*

I came out of the vision in a swoon. "Whoa."

"I think someone else has been drinking," Aaron said. He waved us in. "Come. There are Botox stations in every room. As a bonus, they are doing some lip fillers for a hundred dollars, too." He tried to touch my mouth, and I dodged his fingers. Aaron looked dazed, then he laughed. He cupped his hand around his mouth as if imparting a secret. "Mary enlisted a few doctor and nurse friends from three different clinics in the city to help. Shhh. It's a surprise for everyone."

"Terrific," I said without much enthusiasm.

He widened his eyes. "I've been driving supplies back and forth since Thursday, he said. So, they are fully stocked for all your fine-line needs." Then he smiled. "But soon, I won't ever have to do it anymore."

"Did you get that promotion you were talking about?"

The question seemed to sober Aaron. "Not yet," he grumbled. He shook his head and forced another smile. Even though I knew it was fake, the smile he exhibited actually lit up his eyes. Wow. It took real talent to look happy when you didn't feel it. Either that or Aaron was a sociopath. "You guys better come on in before the good stations get got." He chuckled at his alliteration.

There were at least thirty women and a handful of men in the penthouse suite. I saw Carmen, wearing a flowing red maxi-dress, standing out on the balcony speaking with Nurse Mary. Her hair was down, and the wind blew it around in a way that made her look like she was being filtered through a slow-motion camera.

She looked through the window, her eyes locking with mine, and she waved at me to join her. Perfect. I didn't even have to wait for her to finish her conversation. Also, if her outfit had nothing to do with Samantha's death or what had happened to Blanche, it still bugged me. Why say your ring ripped the pocket if it didn't? Or maybe she'd had her pants off and was retrieving an item from the pocket. It was unlikely. Carmen was righthanded. Even if she hadn't been wearing her jumper when it ripped, it was a stretch to think she'd suddenly start using her left hand for simple tasks.

"I'm going to go talk to Carmen," I told Pippa and Gilly. "You two keep your eyes open but also try to have fun. Gilly, please promise if you do Botox, you don't go overboard. I'm a fan of all your expressions and would like you to be able to continue to use them."

"You're not the boss of me, Nora." She stuck her tongue out. "I'll freeze my face if I want to."

"Do you know that sticking your tongue out can create wrinkles around the edges of your lips? It's almost as bad as sucking on a straw," a woman said. She wore a flowery blouse and white dress pants. "I'd love to talk to you about this new hyaluronic acid filler we're using at New-vow Clinic to take care of those nasty lines."

"I'd love to hear about your product," Gilly said and followed the woman into the dining room.

"She doesn't have any lines around her mouth," I complained.

"You should know better than to tell Gilly not to do something. She's as stubborn as you are." Pippa giggled. "Do you want me to keep an eye on her?"

I grinned at my beautiful friend and all her glow. "You are going to be the best mom in the world."

"I hope so," she said.

"I know so. You're still taking care of me."

She gave me a quick hug. "Don't keep Carmen waiting."

We parted ways, me in the direction of the balcony, and Pippa in the direction of Gilly. I opened the door and heard Nurse Mary say, "We have a bottle missing."

"Do you think someone broke it and was too afraid to confess?" Carmen asked. "Do you have enough for tonight?"

"Yes." Nurse Mary scowled. "The paperwork for missing medication is a pain in the butt. Especially when you can't account for it." She sighed. "Don't worry. I'll get it figured out."

"Oh, hi, Nora. Come on out here," Carmen said. "Mary, this is Nora Black, my predecessor at Belliza Beauty. Without her, the Midwest region would have never lasted."

"How nice," Mary said. "What do you do now, Nora?"

"I own a boutique spa shop in my hometown of Garden Cove."

"This is who you were telling me about," Mary said with a smile. "Let me go get you a card. I'd love to have a conversation with you about your face and skincare products. If they are as good as Carmen says, I'd love to do business with you."

To say I was stunned would be the understatement of the century. Flabbergasted was more like it. "Carmen told you about me?" Was she feeling guilty for taking my job?

"I love your nighttime moisturizer, the one with blue tansy in it. It has really brightened my skin. I don't have to wear near as much makeup as I used to," Carmen told me.

Okay, it was officially freaky Friday. "I had no idea. Did you come to the store when I wasn't there?"

She covered her mouth on a giggle. "No. I had a cousin who was vacationing at one of the resorts down there. I had her pick me up a few things. Besides, I wanted to see what you were up to. You have great products, Nora."

"Uhm, thanks." My tongue felt thick as I tried to process my emotions.

"Carmen and I have been friends for years," Mary added. She lowered her voice. "I still can't believe the way Belliza treated you."

"Mary," Carmen admonished. "Don't."

"She doesn't know?" Mary asked.

I held up my hand. "What don't I know?"

"Carmen made sure Belliza gave you a generous severance package. They wanted her because of me, but she wouldn't say yes until they met her demands."

Carmen blushed. "I should have talked to you first, Nora. But things were happening quickly, and you were dealing with a lot at home. I just didn't want you to get screwed. I'm really sorry that your leave of absence turned into a permanent leave. I tried to get them to make it a two-person job, but they wouldn't."

Lord. I had always thought the severance package was generous. The fact that Belliza included health coverage had been surprising. "The insurance?"

"That was a deal-breaker for me. I know how bad it

can be to try and get independent insurance, and Belliza can afford it."

Impulsively, I hugged Carmen.

She stiffened for a moment, then relaxed and embraced me back. "Does this mean you forgive me?"

My hysterectomy, which had been forty-eight thousand dollars between the surgery, anesthesia, and aftercare, had only cost me three thousand because I'd had the Belliza insurance. Without the severance money, I wouldn't have been able to buy my house or my shop. Without the shop, I wouldn't have Pippa with me, and she wouldn't have met Jordy. How would things have turned out with Gilly and Lloyd had I left Garden Cove before she'd started dating him? And best of all, I had Ezra in my life. I didn't even know why I'd been angry with her in the first place.

"Forgive you? I thank you. You afforded me a life better than I ever imagined."

She grinned, then sniffled as we parted. "Good. I'm delighted to hear it."

Mary patted my shoulder. "It's nice to meet you, Nora. Don't forget to call me." To Carmen, she said, "I'll see you in there." And with that, she left the two of us on the balcony.

"I can't believe you did all that," I said.

Carmen shook her head. "You were a great mentor, Nora. And I might be a bitch in heels, as your friend put it, but I believe women should look out for women."

Now I felt awkward asking her about her jumper because I no longer wanted her to be a suspect. But I asked, anyway. "I loved the red jumper you wore yesterday. Where did you get it?"

"It's from Cali's Way. I like to buy from indie designers, and she makes incredible clothing. She made this dress as a matter of fact. I'll get you the address if you want."

I did want, but that could wait. "I saw Aaron with it this afternoon when he got back from the dry cleaners."

"I don't know why he took it across town. I told him there was a dry cleaner in the hotel."

I glanced down. Carmen's ring was definitely on the left hand. "How'd you get the tear in the pocket?" I was as subtle as a yellow dot on a purple canvas. Frankly, Carmen had thrown me off my game with her revelation.

"I didn't tear my jumper." Her eyes widened in horror. "It's my favorite. I swear I'm going to roast Aaron over an open spit if he ruined my outfit."

I don't know what answer I'd expected, but it wasn't that. Eep. I'd just got Aaron into a heap of hot water. "I think he got it fixed at a tailor. I'm sure it's fine."

"His focus has been way off lately. I've considered letting him go a few times." She shook her head. "It's difficult to train a new assistant, though. Losing Pippa is the only time I've ever begrudged you. She was a gem."

I glanced back into the suite. I couldn't see either Pippa or Gilly, but my thoughts were with them. "Pippa is the best." I smiled sadly. "I'm sorry about Samantha. That must be awful for Gregory."

"You guys dated, right?"

I nodded. "It was a long, long time ago. I don't have any feelings for him if you're concerned."

"No, it's not that. He's just acting...like a man I don't know. He's more upset about that meditation pod than he is about her death. Poor girl. Were you at the launch tonight?"

"Yes." I studied her expression. She seemed unaffected. "You don't know?"

"Know what?"

"There was another incident. The volunteer for the pod demonstration had a terrible reaction. They've taken her to the hospital."

"Christ." She blanched. "I...I was supposed to help Gregory. Oh, God. Maybe I *will* keep Aaron around. He told me there was a crisis that needed my attention up here. I was mad because it was over the catering, and that's something he should be able to handle, but now." She pressed her fingers to her chest. "He might have saved my life."

"The volunteer is still alive." I reminded myself to text Ezra for an update.

"I'm so glad." She glanced over my shoulder toward the suite. "I better get inside. This party is getting ready to start, and I need to talk with all the staff to find out what happened to the missing bottle of Botox."

"The what?"

Carmen heaved a sigh. "That's what Mary was talking about when you came out here. She borrowed twenty vials of Botox from a local clinic, and now one of them is unaccounted for. Someone probably nabbed it thinking they could do a Botox party at home, but that stuff can be dangerous if you don't know what you're doing." She gave me a quick hug. "It really is good to see you again, Nora. I'm glad we got to talk."

I gulped down another swell of emotion. "Me too." I stayed out on the balcony after she departed because I needed a moment to get my feelings squared away. Cripes. I'd been harboring ill will for a woman who had put my life on the right track. I brushed away the guilt. From this moment forward, it would be a clean slate.

The city was alive with beauty, the setting sun washing away the industrial-looking streets as high-rise buildings began to glow with activity. I sucked in a breath then pivoted to face the penthouse. I could see into the kitchen, the living room area, and part of the dining room. I watched as the Botox Brigade lined up at the different stations in the penthouse.

I wondered who would have stolen the missing vial. Had it been broken and hidden? I knew enough about it to know that it was kept in a powder form until the saline was mixed in for injections. Breaking a bottle of that could be dangerous, especially if you inhale the particles.

I saw Aaron, tipsily making his way into the kitchen. He lifted his leather satchel onto the range top and withdrew something silver. Maybe a laptop? The bag spilled sideways, and something pink slid partially out.

Pink. I went rigid. Samantha's tablet had been pink. Did Aaron have it? Had he taken it from Samantha, or had she given it to him? It might not even be the missing tablet. There were other pink things.

The only thing I knew for sure was that I needed to get a look inside Aaron's man-purse.

# CHAPTER 22

*I* went back into the suite and looked for Gilly and Pippa. They were both buried in conversation with Ms. Lip Filler in the dining area. A small crowd of ladies who looked as if they had enough filler in their lips for a lifetime had formed a circle around them.

Pippa, who looked a little green around the gills, peered over at me and gave me a palms-up "did you find something" gesture?

I gave her back a "maybe" shrug. I waved her over because I didn't want to talk around the cast of Unreal Housewives.

She cast a sideways "I'm worried about our girl" glance at Gilly, and I poo-pooed her concern with a downward swipe of my hand. Gilly was an adult with two almost-grown kids and capable of making her own decisions.

I didn't know how to put all that in my body language, so I balled my fists onto my hips and gave her the "just get over here" stare.

She gave me an exasperated nod of "okay" then came over.

"What?" Pippa asked. I didn't need my glasses to see she had a bead of perspiration on her upper lip.

"I think Aaron might have Samantha's tablet. And he is definitely hiding something. Carmen said she spilled wine on her jumper, but she wasn't the one who ripped the pocket."

"Why would he lie about that? And what does he have to gain by stealing Samantha's tablet?"

"That's what I'm trying to figure out. Aaron has his satchel in the kitchen. I think he's stashed it in a cabinet."

Her brow narrowed. "What do you need me to do?"

"Can you distract him?"

Her whole body asked, "WTF?" She frowned at me. "How am I supposed to do that?"

"I don't know. Talk to him about babies, engagements, hopes and dreams."

Pippa rolled her eyes. "That will really keep his attention." She dabbed her upper lip with the back of her hand. "It's extremely warm in here."

"No, it's not. Maybe you should go back to the room. This might be a bit much for you."

That fired her up. "There are women who run freaking marathons until they give birth at the finish line, Nora. I think I can handle distracting one drunk guy."

Speaking of Aaron, he strolled out of the bathroom. He took a few steps, adjusted his belt a notch tighter, then smiled as he joined the party. It was easy to see the effect he had on many of the women in the room. He wasn't my type. I didn't tend to fall for narcissistic liars, but, admittedly, he was easy on the eyes with his perfect bone structure and lean but solid physique.

I patted Pippa's back. "You're up. Don't go anywhere alone with him, though."

"I'm not planning to play seven minutes in heaven with the guy." She wrinkled her nose. "He's a friend, Nora. Well, more like a friendly acquaintance. A fracquaintance, if you will. I really hope you're wrong about his involvement."

My smile was tight as I nodded. "Me too. If Aaron heads to the kitchen, give me a signal."

"Would you like me to caw-caw?"

"Only if you're in the bathroom."

She crossed her arms. "Ha not so ha."

"Shout these words: free Botox!" I told her. "When you both get rushed, it will give me time to get out before he sees me."

"I'm not doing that," she said flatly. "I'll think of something."

I swatted her butt. "Go get him, tiger."

\* \* \*

I HID, sort of, behind Pippa as she made her way to Aaron.

"Hey, Aaron," she said. "I've been looking all over for you."

"You have?" he said with a lopsided grin. "Here I am." He gestured to his torso.

I tried not to snicker but failed as I diverted to the left and headed into the kitchen area. I passed Carmen as she was coming out, and I was going in. We smiled and nodded, and I liked the new way I had of thinking about her. It was as if a weight had been lifted from my soul.

The kitchen was the only room semi-cordoned off from the others, except for the bathrooms and the bedroom. It had a wall in front that opened on both ends, and it was also the only open room without a clinician chair. Instead, the counters were full of cupcakes, including three large trays. One was tagged "vegan", another tagged "low carb", and the last tagged "decadent" aka "loosen up a button" cupcakes.

A woman came in and grabbed a low-carb cupcake. She looked as though she lived on Tic Tacs and crispy water chips. If I was stickpin skinny, I'd have gone for decadent. Come to think of it, that's probably why I wasn't that thin. She grabbed a club soda from a tub filled with a variety of drinks. I saw ginger ale, so I grabbed one for Pippa and a Diet Coke for Gilly and put them on the counter.

As soon as the woman vacated, I started opening cabinets, both upper and lower.

Bingo!

The satchel was in the lower cabinet under the stove-top. I'd have crouched to search the damn thing, but if I had to make a break for it, I wasn't sure if my knees would cooperate. I looked around quickly to make sure I wasn't being watched, then seized the satchel and took it to the counter behind the partition.

Before I could look inside, my phone beeped. I ignored it for expediency. I turned up the flap and saw a silver laptop, a tablet, several pens, and a pink phone.

Huh. Did Aaron own a pink phone, or was this Samantha's missing phone?

I lifted it up, and I could make out a unicorn sticker on the back of the case, just like the one that had been on her tablet. This had to be Samantha's. I took a chance and put it in my purse. Unless Aaron was looking for it, he probably wouldn't notice it was missing until I was long gone.

A familiar aroma wafted up from the bag: cedarwood and eucalyptus.

*"A deal's a deal," a man says. He tugs down on the brim of his hat. "I took care of the pod." He's wearing jeans and a t-shirt. Aaron.*

*"Good. If it all goes well," the other man, who I was sure now was Brian Langford, added, "you will be sitting in a corner office in no time."*

*They stood on a balcony because the city skyline was in view, and their only audience, a sleeping quarter moon.*

*"I had to talk Remy off the ledge. She's going to blow this for both of us. I'm afraid she's going to do something that will expose us."*

*"I'll worry about Remy," Langford says. "You just make sure that launch doesn't happen."*

Cripes. Aaron was working for Selebrate's enemy. I rummaged the bottom of the satchel, and my fingers hit cloth and something firmer—a hat with a stiff brim. Just like I'd seen in the vision of Samantha with her lover.

My throat grew tight as I swallowed a knot that had formed. Aaron and Samantha had been lovers. How had I not recognized him in the first vision I'd had of the unfortunate girl? Crap. He'd had a hat in the gin and lime vision as well.

"Wait," I heard Pippa say too late, as Aaron wandered into the kitchen.

His mouth dropped open, then his eyes hardened as he saw me holding his hat in hand. "What are you doing with my stuff, Nora?"

"I..." I struggled to come up with a feasible explanation. "It was on the counter when I came in." I dropped his hat and turned around to grab the Diet Coke and ginger ale. "I came in for drinks for Gilly and Pippa. Pippa hasn't been feeling too good."

"I know," he said. "She barfed on my shoes."

I glanced down to see hours-old guacamole and Mexican fried ice cream glop on Aaron's very expensive loafers.

"Oops."

He shoved his hat in his bag and crossed to the sink, turning on the water and wetting several paper towels. "Damn it." He scrubbed the puke off his shoes, but some of it was sticking to the stitching.

"Sorry," Pippa said. "I really am." She took the ginger ale from me, and we hastily made a retreat back to the living quarters.

When we were safely amongst people, I whispered, "I've got Samantha's phone."

"You what?" Pippa asked.

"There was a pink phone in the bag that matched her tablet." I motioned at Gilly. "Let's go take a look at it in the bathroom."

Gilly joined us, and all three of us went into the bathroom. Pippa locked the door behind us.

My bestie Pippa still looked almost green. "You threw up on him, huh?"

"Yep." She groaned. "I could've made it in here, or to a trashcan or something, but instead, I barfed on his shoes. I didn't want to take a chance he'd go into the kitchen. But then I'd grabbed some napkins to clean up the floor, and he was already heading your way." She pressed her palm against her chest. "I don't know if my heart can take all this cloak and dagger business."

"I finished cleaning up the mess," Gilly said. "You're welcome."

"Oh, Gilly, I'm sorry." Pippa was on the verge of tears again.

"Don't even worry about it. I have twins, which means I've been pissed on, pooped on, and puked on ten ways to Sunday. It's no big deal. You'll see." She chucked Pippa under the chin then looked at me. "Why are we hiding in the bathroom?"

I pulled the pink phone from my purse. "Ta-dah."

"Nice," Gilly said. "Since when do you like pink?"

"It's not mine. I'm pretty sure it's Samantha Jones' phone. I found it in Aaron's satchel."

Gilly paled. "You went through Aaron's satchel?"

Oh, right. She was mid filler talk when Pippa and I had come up with the plan.

"He had it in there. Also, in a vision, I saw that he and Samantha were lovers."

Gilly blew out a surprised breath.

Then I dropped the next smell-o-vision bomb, "And

he's working for Brian Langford to sabotage Selebrate and the Stress-less Meditation Pod."

It was Pippa's turn to gasp. "That's corporate espionage. He could do prison time for that."

"I know!" I squeaked.

"What about Samantha?" Gilly asked. "Did you see what happened to her?"

"No," I said. "I didn't get any hits on her death." My phone beeped again. I took it out of my purse. "It's from Ezra. Hold on." I unlocked the screen with my finger and checked my messages. I held it at arm's length away from my face. "Crap."

Pippa took it from me. She read the messages, then said, "Blanche isn't doing well. She's not responding to any of the medicine they are giving her at the hospital. They are doing high doses of steroids now, and they've put in a breathing tube."

"Oh no," Pippa said. "We should go see her."

I nodded. "We'll do Blanche the most good, though, if we can figure out what made her sick in the first place."

"Maybe you should go down and sniff around the launch display," Gilly said. "Maybe there's a memory there that you haven't yet seen."

We heard several startled shouts out in the room. A sharp scream froze the three of us in place. Whatever was going on out there, we were safest in a locked room. "Text Ezra, and tell him to get Luke and get up here ASAP." I slowly unlocked the door.

"What are you doing?" Gilly hissed.

"I just want to take a quick peek. We can lock it right back up again." I turned the knob and eased the door open a crack. My stomach dropped. I closed the door and locked it again.

Aaron had Carmen in a chokehold, and he held a syringe to her throat.

I heard him bellow, "What did you do with my stuff?"

Crap. Crap. He had discovered the missing phone, and for some reason, he thought Carmen was the culprit.

"Tell Ezra to call the police. We have a hostage situation now."

# CHAPTER 23

*I* heard Mary telling everyone to get out, even as Aaron was yelling at her to shut up. Carmen was crying, scared and confused. All I could think about was her telling me that women needed to help each other, and how I was responsible for her current lethal situation. She'd been in the kitchen before me, and I'd told Aaron that I'd found his satchel open on the counter.

He'd believed me, apparently, but now Carmen was paying the price. If he wanted the phone, he could have it. In exchange for Carmen's life.

I grabbed the pink phone, slid it into my pocket, then unlocked the door.

"Don't," Gilly said. "Don't go out there."

"I have to. I'll show Aaron the phone and offer it to him, anything to keep him distracted and to keep him from killing Carmen until the cavalry arrives." I prayed it would work. Soon, Ezra and Luke would arrive, and shortly after, the cops. I only needed to stop him from hurting Carmen, and the good guys could take him down later. "Here, give me my phone." I took it from Pippa and turned on the record feature. I used it all the time when I was crafting new recipes because it was easier than writing down what I was doing. I turned it on and slid my phone into my purse.

"Don't," Pippa said, grabbing my shirt.

"I have to, Pippa. Lock the door when I'm out." I jerked out of her grasp, the fabric on my sleeve tearing as I bolted out the bathroom door and slammed it shut behind me.

Carmen stared at me, her eyes wild and pleading as Aaron dragged her back toward the bedroom.

"Aaron," I snapped.

He stopped and stared at me.

"All I did was ask you what you did to my red outfit," Carmen said. "I didn't take anything."

"You know," he said. "I know you know." Aaron's words slurred, and he began to sound like someone who'd gone a few too many days without sleep.

"Let her go," I said calmly as I set my purse on the floor.

"No," he said. "She has my property, and I want it back."

"You mean Samantha's property?" I asked as I withdrew the phone from my pocket and showed it to him. I kept a reasonable distance between us because I didn't want him to surprise me. Cripes, where was the cavalry?

Aaron snarled, jerking Carmen backward, the needle mere centimeters from the pulse beating in her neck.

"Stop it!" Mary said. "You're hurting her."

"That's the point." Aaron's wild gaze landed on the phone. "Give that to me. Or you can watch Carmen die."

"You mean the same way Samantha did? Why'd you kill her?"

The question shocked him into stillness. Carmen's eyes widened. "Oh, my God. Aaron? You killed Gregory's assistant?"

"More than that," I said. "Samantha was his lover. Poor girl. She had no idea what a sociopathic boyfriend she had." I dangled the phone between two fingers. "I wonder why you kept her phone. Something to remember her by?"

I saw Aaron swallow, his gaze practically melded to the phone. "Give that to me." He allowed the needle to puncture Carmen's skin. Her eyes bugged, and she gagged on a squeak. "You don't know squat, Nora." Aaron's eyes took on that glazed stare again. I thought it had just been alcohol, but now I wondered if he'd taken some kind of drug as well.

I'd had enough visions and clues to what might have happened. At the very least, enough to freak him out so that Aaron was focused on me and not Carmen. So, I kept talking, because as long as he was listening, he wasn't trying to kill Carmen. Or me, for that matter.

"You sabotaged the Stress-less Pod," I said. "Probably Wednesday night. And you did it for Brian Langford. You're working for him in exchange for a job. Junior executive, right?"

"How could you..." His grip around Carmen's neck loosened. "You can't know that."

"You had no idea that Samantha was spying on Langford for Gregory, so you didn't count on her finding out about your plans to sabotage the Stress-less pod. Maybe she thought about how if you were willing to betray your boss— you might betray her, too? Or did she love you too much to think you'd want money and prestige more than you wanted her?" I gripped the phone, wishing it was Aaron's neck. What a snake. "I bet she has all kinds of recordings on this phone. You couldn't crack the passcode, could you? Destroying the phone wouldn't destroy the automatic backups to the cloud." I lifted the phone. "I have the same model. Everything on this thing is downloaded to my personal cloud. You have to use the phone's app to delete anything from the cloud."

"Impossible." He shook his head. "Did Langford tell you? Did he flip on me? Coward," Aaron cried out. "He's a damn coward."

A pounding at the door startled him enough for his hand to drop away from Carmen's neck. Carmen, aka the Bitch in Heels, swung her elbow back into Aaron's stomach. He staggered back, and then Carmen stomped so hard on his foot, that her stiletto sank into the soft Italian leather and pierced his flesh.

He screamed as he fell backward.

Mary and I rushed forward. Mary pried the injection from his hand, then Carmen and I pushed him flat onto the floor. I heard the little air left in his lungs whoosh out as I sat on his chest.

Hard.

Carmen did the same, her bony butt sinking like sword points into his groin. He yelped and groaned.

"What an asshat," she said.

"Yeah," I agreed. "I think he's fired."

"Security," Luke hollered.

"I'll open the door," said Mary. She accidentally kicked Aaron in the hip. And by accidentally, I mean on purpose. I was sure her wedge heel would leave quite the bruise.

"You stole the Botox, didn't you?" I asked Aaron.

"You can't...prove it." He stared at me, eyes bulging. "Get. Off. Me."

"Oh, my God," breathed Carmen. "He took the missing vial."

"Yes," I said. "I'm afraid Aaron used it to kill Samantha Jones."

"How?" Carmen asked.

I stared down at Aaron. "You mixed the powdered Botox with the aromatherapy. The lemon verbena, didn't you?"

His lips pressed together.

I was only guessing now, but I figured it had to be the truth. "You held Samantha down using Carmen's red jumper. And she tore the pocket, right? And you held her there until she died."

"I didn't want to kill her..." he wheezed. "...believe me."

I shook my head. "And now, because of you, a sweet woman named Blanche, who volunteered to get in that death machine, is now on a ventilator in the hospital. She's dying because of you."

"Accident," he managed through gritted teeth. "I didn't mean for anyone else to get hurt. I thought the launch would be canceled." He weakly flailed his arms, but whatever energy he'd had before was flattened, literally, by two pissed-off women. He stopped trying to move.

"You didn't do anything to stop Blanche's poisoning, and you had planned Samantha's death," I seethed, my rage bubbling to the surface. "You timed it, Aaron. Made sure you poisoned her right after she ate the fugu. So it would look like an accident. That's premeditation, and that means murder in the first degree. You do know our state has the death penalty, right? Turn yourself in, give evidence against Langford. If you cooperate, you might only get life. That's better than no life."

Luke, Ezra, and Jordy spilled into the room, along with half a dozen cops and security staff.

Mary rushed to the nearest Botox station and grabbed another vial. She showed it to Luke. "This is pyridostigmine. It's an antidote for Botox, sort of. It reverses the effects by relaxing the muscles, but it will take a few hours to completely take effect. Someone needs to get this to the hospital, since they probably don't have it on hand, and tell them Blanche was poisoned by aerosolized Botox."

"You ladies can get off him," said Luke. "He's going to be arrested now."

"For murder," I said. "And attempted murder."

Ezra grabbed my hands to help me to my feet, and Luke did the same for Carmen.

"My word against yours," spat Aaron as two uniformed officers dragged him to a standing position.

I lifted my phone out of my purse. "Recorded every word. Like I said, I have the same phone as the woman you killed."

They took Aaron out of the room, and I collapsed into Ezra's arms. For a spa weekend, this had turned out to be the least relaxing weekend of my entire life.

"Pippa!" Jordy shouted. "Where is she?"

Pippa and Gilly ran out of the bathroom. Pippa launched herself at Jordy. "I'm okay," she said. "I'm fine."

Luke was checking Gilly over.

"Are you okay?" Ezra asked softly as he held me tightly.

"No," I told him. "No, I'm not. But I will be."

* * *

SATURDAY, *August 9th...*

We'd spent three hours at the police station giving witness statements, then two hours at the hospital to check in on Blanche. I promised Blanche we'd do a podcast together when she recovered, and even with the tube down her throat, it seemed to lift her spirits. I'd feared for Blanche's life, and I was so grateful to the universe that she'd survived.

The police had taken Langford, Aaron, and Gregory in for questioning. I hoped all three of them went to jail for a long, long time. As far as I was concerned, they were the real villains. Their greed and their need to win, to beat each other to market, had been the catalyst for one death and one near miss.

Carmen had broken off her engagement with Gregory in a spectacular manner by throwing her ring at him as he was being escorted down the hallway. I'd already changed my mind about Carmen before then. However, her swift decision to dump the scummy bastard had raised her even higher in my esteem. Life was too short to settle for toxic people.

Nurse Mary had given me her card, and we made an informal arrangement for a business call in a few weeks. The idea of branching out my sales scared the bejeezus out of me. But it opened up so many possibilities for the future of Scents & Scentsability and the people I love. Especially now that Pippa was getting married and having a baby.

The pod was being tested to confirm the toxin for evidence in the murder of Samantha Jones. I'd found out from Jackson, the engineer, that there was no easy way to drain the aromatherapy. Since each had its own holder, the design team hadn't thought it was necessary. I shuddered to think what would have happened to Blanche if she hadn't been removed from the pod so quickly, or if she hadn't received medical help right away. The results of her exposure would have been fatal.

Jordy and Ezra had gotten separate rooms at the Marlon Hotel, so Pippa and I joined our fellas. Not for anything sexy, we were all too tired for that. We only agreed to leave Gilly, though, when she'd said she wouldn't be sleeping alone, either.

Also, I'd asked my BFFs if we could leave the convention early. I really just wanted to go home at this point. Gilly wanted to stay for obvious reasons, so we were leaving her the car, and Pippa and I were driving home in the afternoon with Ezra and Jordy. The only real bummer for me was that I'd been looking forward to the Roaring

Twenties theme party. I bought the outfit and everything, and now I'd probably never get a chance to wear it.

Ezra and I had finally gotten to bed around five-thirty in the morning, and I was ready to call my birthday officially canceled.

I awoke at noon, warm and snuggled in against Ezra's chest. He was awake when I opened my eyes and peeked up at him. "Morning," I said.

"Happy Birthday," he told me.

I groaned. "Don't remind me." I grabbed a pillow from behind me and put it over my head, determined to stay there until the day was done. My bladder had other ideas. "Be right back."

I rolled out of bed, not bothering to put on clothes, and walked to the bathroom. Ezra had seen me plenty in my birthday suit, and I no longer tried to hide any of my flaws from him.

"I hate for you to leave, but I love to watch you go," he said as I looked back at him.

I brushed my teeth because while sexy time had been off the table early in the morning, I was willing to reexamine the merits of it this afternoon.

When I came out of the bathroom, Ezra was propped up on his elbow, sporting his own birthday suit.

"All right," I growled. "Happy Birthday to me."

I crawled back into bed with him. He drew me into his arms, the heat of his body searing my skin with pleasure. He kissed my ear. My whole body hummed.

"I love you, Nora Black."

"I love you, Ezra Holden," I said. I stared into his

emerald eyes as I laced my fingers with his. "You are the best present I've ever had."

"I even come unwrapped," he said.

My eyes widened.

He laughed. "I didn't mean it like it sounded."

"That's okay. I like you unwrapped." And with that, he melted me with a kiss I felt to my core. Then, he made love to me until every lousy thing that had happened over the past two days fell away.

* * *

WE STAYED in bed as long as possible, until we got an urgent text from Gilly, saying that she needed us in the lobby of the Frazier.

"Crap. I hope the hotel isn't trying to kick Gilly out. None of this stuff was our fault," I said as I threw on my clothes.

Ezra and I hurried across the street, and Gilly met us at the door. "Come on," she said. "Hurry."

"What's going on?" I couldn't keep the panic out of my voice. "Is it Pippa? What's wrong?" I hoped the stress hadn't done anything to the baby. I mean, I didn't think pregnancy worked that way, but what did I know?

Gilly grabbed my hand and tugged me. "Just come on."

So, I went with her. Ezra looked as calm as could be as he followed us a few feet behind. He was so good in a crisis. Another thing I loved about him.

We passed the elevators. "Are we going up?"

"Nope," Gilly said. "We're almost there."

"Where?"

"Right here," she said, smiling now. We were standing outside Darbie's, the restaurant I'd wanted to eat at all weekend.

"It's closed," I complained.

Luke popped his head out. "Ah, you're here. Everything's ready." He gave Gilly a kiss on the cheek, then opened the door all the way. Luke wore pinstripe gangster pants, a white collared shirt with a bow tie and suspenders. And were those spats over his shoes?

Pippa and Jordy appeared from behind Luke, dressed as a mobster and gun moll, and they all yelled, including Ezra, "Happy Birthday!"

"I am really underdressed," I said. Hell, I barely combed my hair, let alone put on makeup.

"I have your clothes, makeup, and everything. We'll get put together while the chef prepares your birthday dinner."

We all walked inside the restaurant, and there was a single table for eight, decorated in gold and black, with "Roaring 20s" on the napkins and the party hats. "How did you guys make this happen?" It couldn't have been preplanned.

"I know the chef," Luke said. He smiled. "Darbie!" he yelled. A black woman, with a white and black chef jacket and a black chef hat, came out of the kitchen. I recognized her from her picture in *Midwest Wine and Food* magazine.

"I'm cooking," she yelled back.

Luke laughed. "Come over and meet the birthday girl."

Darbie strolled toward us with the confidence that comes with being a James Beard award-winning cook.

"Darbie Jenkins, meet Nora Black."

The name struck me. Could it be? Luke promised to look after Michael Jenkins' family. He'd mentioned a Dee. Was it Darbie? I looked at Luke, and he nodded. This had to be Michael's wife.

She thrust out her hand. "Happy Birthday, Nora. Any friend of Luke's is a friend of mine. I've heard you've had a harrowing few days, so I hope my food can brighten your soul."

"And I've read a lot about you," I said with a wide smile. "I've been dying to eat here."

"It's tastier if you manage to stay alive," she joked. Then grimaced. "That was said poorly."

"Staying alive is better than the alternative," I assured her.

Darbie went back into the kitchen, and Luke took me aside. "Keller and Langford have both been officially charged. Between Samantha's phone and Aaron's laptop, the feds had enough to formally charge both of them with corporate espionage. I think the local prosecutor is pushing to link them to Samantha's death and Blanche's near miss. Either way, they are going to be punished."

"And Gregory?"

"They don't have enough evidence to hold him on anything, but I think he'll be under a microscope for a long, long while."

"Thanks for telling me." I'd wanted them in jail, but it was a pale kind of justice for the harm they'd caused.

Gilly tugged on me from the front as Pippa pushed me from behind.

"Come on, Nora," Gilly said. "Time to get us dressed for the party."

"What about Ezra?" I asked.

"He's got a change of clothes, too," Pippa said as we walked to the restaurant bathroom.

Gilly grinned. "And after our little party, we've got massages and facials to finish off the celebration."

Pippa jumped in, "And if you still want to go home after all that, we'll get in the vehicles and go, but if you don't, the hotel manager is comping us two more suites. We could all have our own rooms." She wiggled her brows.

How could I say no to any of that? So, instead, I said, "Yes, absolutely."

"This is going to be the best birthday ever!" Gilly said as she threw her arms around me. We grabbed Pippa in to complete our circle.

"Best friends ever," I told them.

I looked over my shoulder to Ezra, who was smiling as he watched us. He mouthed, *I love you*. I mouthed it back.

"I'm so flippin' lucky," I told my BFFs. "Now, let's get dressed up. We have so much to celebrate."

The End

PIT PERFECT MURDER

BARKSIDE OF THE MOON COZY MYSTERIES
BOOK 1

When cougar-shifter Lily Mason moves to Moonrise, Missouri, she wishes for only three things from the town and its human population. . . to find a job, to find a place to live, and to live as a human, not a therianthrope.

Lily gets more than she bargains for when a rescue pit

bull named Smooshie rescues her from an oncoming car, and it's love at first sight. Thanks to Smooshie, Lily's first two wishes are granted by Parker Knowles, the owner of the Pit Bull Rescue center, who offers her a job at the shelter and the room over his garage for rent.

Lily's new life as an integrator is threatened when Smooshie finds Katherine Kapersky, the local church choir leader and head of the town council, dead in the field behind the rescue center. Unfortunately, there are more suspects than mourners for the elderly town leader. Can Lily keep her less-than-human status under wraps? Or will the killer, who has pulled off a nearly Pit Perfect murder, expose her to keep Lily and her dog from digging up the truth?

## Chapter One

**When I was eighteen years** old, I came home from a sleepover and found my mom and dad with their throats cut, and their hearts ripped from their chests.

My little brother Danny was in a broom closet in the kitchen, his arms wrapped around his knees, and his face pale and ghostly. Until that day, I'd planned to go to college and study medicine after graduation, but instead, I ended up staying home and taking care of my seven-year-old brother.

Seventeen years later, my brother was murdered. At the time, Danny's death looked like it would go unsolved, much like my parents' had.

Without Haze Kinsey, my best friend since we were five, the killers would have gotten away with it. She was a special agent for the FBI for almost a decade, and when I called her about Danny's death, she dropped everything to come help me get him justice. The evil group of witches and Shifters responsible for the decimation of my family paid with their lives.

Yes. I said witches and Shifters. Did I forget to mention I'm a werecougar? Oh, and my friend Hazel is a witch. Recently, I discovered witches in my own family tree on my mother's side. Shifters, in general, only mated with Shifters, but witches were the exception. As a matter of fact, my friend Haze is mated to a bear Shifter.

I wouldn't have known about the witch in my genealogy, though, if a rogue witch coven hadn't done some funky hoodoo witchery to me. Apparently, the spell activated a latent talent that had been dormant in my hybrid genes.

My ancestor's magic acted like truth serum to anyone who came near her. No one could lie in her presence. Lucky me, my ability was a much lesser form of hers. People didn't have to tell me the truth, but whenever they were around me, they had the compulsion to overshare all sorts of private matters about themselves. This can get seriously uncomfortable for all parties involved. Like, the fact that I didn't need to know that Janet Strickland had been wearing the same pair of underwear for an entire week, or that Mike Dandridge had sexual fantasies about clowns.

My newfound talent made me unpopular and unwelcome in a town full of paranormal creatures who thrived on little deceptions. So, when Haze discovered the whereabouts of my dad's brother, a guy I hadn't known even existed, I sold all my belongings, let the bank have my parents' house, jumped in my truck, and headed south.

After two days and 700 miles of nonstop gray, snowy weather, I pulled my screeching green and yellow mini-truck into an auto repair shop called The Rusty Wrench. Much like my beloved pickup, I'd needed a new start, and moving to a small town occupied by humans seemed the best shot. I'd barely made it to Moonrise, Missouri before my truck began its death throes. The vehicle protested the last 127 miles by sputtering to a halt as I rolled her into the closest spot.

The shop was a small white-brick building with a one-car garage off to the right side. A black SUV and a white compact car occupied two of the six parking spots.

A sign on the office door said: *No Credit Cards. Cash Only. Some Local Checks Accepted (Except from Earl—You Know Why, Earl! You check-bouncing bastard).*

A man in stained coveralls, wiping a greasy tool with a rag, came out the side door of the garage. He had a full head of wavy gray hair, bushy eyebrows over light blue, almost colorless eyes, and a minimally lined face that made me wonder about his age. I got out of the truck to greet him.

"Can I help you, miss?" His voice was soft and raspy with a strong accent that was not quite Deep South.

"Yes, please." I adjusted my puffy winter coat. "The heater stopped working first. Then the truck started jerking for the last fifty miles or so."

He scratched his stubbly chin. "You could have thrown a rod, sheared the distributor, or you have a bad ignition module. That's pretty common on these trucks."

I blinked at him. I could name every muscle in the human body and twelve different kinds of viruses, but I didn't know a spark plug from a radiator cap. "And that all means..."

"If you threw a rod, the engine is toast. You'll need a new vehicle."

"Crap." I grimaced. "What if it's the other thingies?"

The scruffy mechanic shrugged. "A sheared distributor is an easy fix, but I have to order in the part, which means it won't get fixed for a couple of days. Best-case scenario, it's the ignition module. I have a few on hand. Could get you going in a couple of hours, but..." he looked over my shoulder at the truck and shook his head, "...I wouldn't get your hopes up."

I must've looked really forlorn because the guy said, "It might not need any parts. Let me take a look at it first. You can grab a cup of coffee across the street at Langdon's One-Stop."

He pointed to the gas station across the road. It didn't look like much. The pale-blue paint on the front of the building looked in need of a new coat, and the weather-beaten sign with the store's name on it had seen better days. There was a car at the gas pumps and a couple more in the parking lot, but not enough to call it busy.

I'd had enough of one-stops, though, thank you. The bathrooms had been horrible enough to make a wereraccoon yark, and it took a lot to make those garbage eaters sick. Besides, I wasn't just passing through Moonrise, Missouri.

"Have you ever heard of The Cat's Meow Café?" Saying the name out loud made me smile the way it had when Hazel had first said it to me. I'd followed my GPS into town, so I knew I wasn't too far away from the place.

"Just up the street about two blocks, take a right on Sterling Street. You can't miss it. I should have some news in about an hour or so, but take your time."

"Thank you, Mister..."

"Greer." He shoved the tool in his pocket. "Greer Knowles."

"I'm Lily Mason."

"Nice to meet ya," said Greer. "The place gets hoppin' around noon. That's when church lets out."

I looked at my phone. It was a little before noon now. "Good. I could go for something to eat. How are the burgers?"

"Best in town," he quipped.

I laughed. "Good enough."

Even in the sub-freezing temperature, my hands were sweating in my mittens. I wasn't sure what had me more nervous, leaving the town I grew up in for the first time in my life or meeting an uncle I'd never known existed.

I crossed a four-way intersection. One of the signs was missing, and I saw the four-by-four post had snapped off at its base. I hadn't noticed it on my way in. Crap. Had I run a stop sign? I walked the two blocks to Sterling. The diner was just where Greer had said. A blue truck, a green mini-coup, and a sheriff's SUV were parked out front.

An alarm dinged as the glass door opened to The Cat's Meow. Inside, there was a row of six booths along the wall, four tables that seated four out in the open floor, and counter seating with about eight cushioned black stools. The interior décor was rustic country with orange tabby kitsch everywhere. A man in blue jeans and a button-down shirt with a string tie sat in the nearest booth. A female police officer sat at a counter chair sipping coffee and eating a cinnamon roll. Two elderly women, one with snowball-white hair, the other a dyed strawberry-blonde, sat in a back booth.

The white poof-headed lady said, "This egg is not over-medium."

"Well, call the mayor," said Redhead. "You're unhappy with your eggs. Again."

"See this?" She pointed at the offending egg. "Slime, right here. Egg snot. You want to eat it?"

"If it'll make you shut up about breakfast food, I'll eat it and lick the plate."

A man with copper-colored hair and a thick beard, tall and well-muscled, stepped out of the kitchen. He wore a white apron around his waist, and he had on a black T-shirt and blue jeans. He held a plate with a single fried egg shining in the middle.

The old woman with the snowy hair blushed, her thin skin pinking up as he crossed the room to their table. "Here you go, Opal. Sorry 'bout the mix-up on your egg." He slid the plate in front of her. "This one is pure perfection." He grinned, his broad smile shining. "Just like you." He winked.

Opal giggled.

The redhead rolled her eyes. "You're as easy as the eggs."

"Oh, Pearl. You're just mad he didn't flirt with you."

As the women bickered over the definition of flirting, the cook glanced at me. He seemed startled to see me there. "You can sit anywhere," he said. "Just pick an open spot."

"I'm actually looking for someone," I told him.

"Who?"

"Daniel Mason." Saying his name gave me a hollow ache. My parents had named my brother Daniel, which told me my dad had loved his brother, even if he didn't speak about him.

The man's brows rose. "And why are you looking for him?"

I immediately knew he was a werecougar like me. The scent was the first clue, and his eyes glowing, just for a second, was another. "You're Daniel Mason, aren't you?"

He moved in closer to me and whispered barely audibly, but with my Shifter senses, I heard him loud and clear. "I go by Buzz these days."

"Who's your new friend, Buzz?" the policewoman asked. Now that she was looking up from her newspaper, I could see she was young.

He flashed a charming smile her way. "Never you mind, Nadine." He gestured to a waitress, a middle-aged woman with sandy-colored hair, wearing a black T-shirt and a blue jean skirt. "Top off her coffee, Freda. Get Nadine's mind on something other than me."

"That'll be a tough 'un, Buzz." Freda laughed. "I don't think Deputy Booth comes here for the cooking."

"More like the cook," the elderly lady with the light strawberry-blonde hair said. She and her friend cackled.

The policewoman's cheeks turned a shade of crimson that flattered her chestnut-brown hair and pale complexion. "Y'all mind your P's and Q's."

Buzz chuckled and shook his head. He turned his attention back to me. "Why is a pretty young thing like you interested in plain ol' me?"

I detected a slight apprehension in his voice.

"If you're Buzz Mason, I'm Lily Mason, and you're my uncle."

The man narrowed his dark-emerald gaze at me. "I think we'd better talk in private."

**Want more? Got to www.**
**barksideofthemoonmysteries.com**

PARANORMAL MYSTERIES &
ROMANCES

BY RENEE GEORGE

**Nora Black Midlife Psychic Mysteries**
www.norablackmysteries.com
Sense & Scent Ability (Book 1)
For Whom the Smell Tolls (Book 2)
War of the Noses (Book 3)
Aroma With A View (Book 4) Coming in 2021

**Peculiar Mysteries**
www.peculiarmysteries.com
You've Got Tail (Book 1) FREE Download
My Furry Valentine (Book 2)
Thank You For Not Shifting (Book 3)
My Hairy Halloween (Book 4)
In the Midnight Howl (Book 5)
My Peculiar Road Trip (Magic & Mayhem) (Book 6)
Furred Lines (Book 7)
My Wolfy Wedding (Book 8)
Who Let The Wolves Out? (Book 9)

My Thanksgiving Faux Paw (Book 10)

## Witchin' Impossible Cozy Mysteries
www.witchinimpossible.com
Witchin' Impossible (Book 1)
Rogue Coven (Book 2)
Familiar Protocol (Booke 3)
Mr & Mrs. Shift (Book 4)

## Barkside of the Moon Mysteries
www.barksideofthemoonmysteries.com
Pit Perfect Murder (Book 1)
Murder & The Money Pit (Book 2)
The Pit List Murders (Book 3)
Pit & Miss Murder (Book 4)
The Prune Pit Murder (Book 5)

## Madder Than Hell
www.madder-than-hell.com
Gone With The Minion (Book 1)
Devil On A Hot Tin Roof (Book 2)
A Street Car Named Demonic (Book 3)

## Hex Drive
https://www.renee-george.com/hex-drive-series
Hex Me, Baby, One More Time (Book 1)
Oops, I Hexed It Again (Book 2)
I Want Your Hex (Book 3)
Hex Me With Your Best Shot (Book 4)

## Midnight Shifters

www.midnightshifters.com
Midnight Shift (Book 1)
The Bear Witch Project (Book 2)
A Door to Midnight (Book 3)
A Shade of Midnight (Book 4)
Midnight Before Christmas (Book 5)

# ABOUT THE AUTHOR

I am a USA Today Bestselling author who writes paranormal mysteries and romances because I love all things whodunit, Otherworldly, and weird. Also, I wish my pittie, the adorable Kona Princess Warrior, and my beagle, Josie the Incontinent Princess, could talk. Or at least be more like Scooby-Doo and help me unmask villains at the haunted house up the street.

When I'm not writing about mystery-solving were-cougars or the adventures of a hapless psychic living among shapeshifters, I am preyed upon by stray kittens who end up living in my house because I can't say no to those sweet, furry faces. (Someone stop telling them where I live!)

I live in Mid-Missouri with my family and I spend my non-writing time doing really cool stuff...like watching TV and cleaning up dog poop

**Follow Renee!**
Bookbub
Renee's Rebel Readers FB Group
Newsletter